Adrift in Soho

a novel by
Colin Wilson

New London Editions

Adrift in Soho
by Colin Wilson

Published in 2011 by New London Editions,
an imprint of Five Leaves Publications,
PO Box 8786, Nottingham NG1 9AW
www.fiveleaves.co.uk

First published in the UK
by Victor Gollancz in 1961

ISBN 973-1-907869-13-6

Five Leaves
acknowledges financial support
from Arts Council England

Typeset and designed by
Four Sheets Design and Print
Printed in Great Britain

Prologue

WHEN I, HARRY PRESTON, was thrown out of the RAF I received (for some reason I have now forgotten) two months' discharge pay. Perhaps they were glad to be rid of me. So I found myself back in civilian life with some kind of capital. I had never owned such a sum before; its possibilities seemed enormous. One obvious use for the money was to pay my mother for twenty weeks ahead (I paid her two pounds a week for my board), and take five months of penurious leisure. In that time I could write a great play or a great novel; I could accustom myself to a rigorous discipline of authorship, writing for six hours a day in the local reference library and eating sandwiches for lunch. I could walk through the streets as the dusk fell and the neon lighting came on in the factories, and listen to the pounding of machinery and smell the leather smell or the steel-drilling smell or the odour of oiled wood. In such moments one savours the intangible nature of freedom, placed for a moment between two worlds and confined by neither. (Why else is it that you will always find a crowd gathered at a building site? Especially if it is demolition work that's going on, offering in the same moment the pleasure of freedom and of vicarious destruction.)

Nothing came of this idea. Two days in the local reference library bored me. The play I wanted to start jammed firmly. I sat there, surrounded by the noise of turning pages and creaking shoes and the smell of leather and polish, and contemplated the infinity of possibilities that lay in the blank pile of foolscap in front of me. Then I re-read a few pages of *Major Barbara,* and wondered at the precision and lightness of every sentence. How was such precision achieved in a desert of freedom? The old lady opposite snuffled and muttered and blew her nose. I found my eyes straying to the plain but nevertheless desirable girl who worked behind the enquiries desk. I had known her slightly at school; it was a temptation to start a conversation. (She always smiled at me when I came in.) But what should I say anyway? The few subjects that interested me intensely would bore her. I jerked myself back to the blank sheet in front of me, and realised how far I had allowed my attention to stray. Discipline... that was it. Discipline over the attention and sexual desire.... That was all very well, but *what* did you discipline? I could concentrate my attention on the page until I felt like busting, ignoring the sniffing of the old lady and refusing to look up when the girl climbed the three steps that enabled her to reach the top shelves. But I hadn't even begun. The paper was still blank. No amount of discipline could produce the rising certainty that would trace lines across the paper with the inevitability of a temperature chart. Human life seemed to reflect the same problem. There was no doubt in my mind that certain lives bear a stamp of futility, while others seem cast in the form of a drama written by a good playwright; like a work of art, they contain an inner logic. That inner logic could form like a crystal in the smell of leather blowing from a factory at nightfall; but how could it be incorporated into the tasteless substance of everyday life?

I spent ten of my forty pounds discovering that a play could not be written by tossing words on to a page like dice, hoping for a double six. Then I felt a sudden miser's desire to recover the ten pounds I'd spent; it would give an illusion of not having wasted a fortnight. So I visited the local employment exchange one morning and asked for a job. It was a wet October day, and my shoes needed repairing. The streets were crowded. I took a short cut through a department store and imagined what it would be like to work there, to be one of the boys in blue overalls who were dragging tea-chests up from the basement. Suddenly I felt like a trapped animal. There was no way out of it. I had been born into a 'free society', an enlightened society, where no great harm could come to its citizens. If I stole a loaf of bread, like Jean Valjean, I should not be punished barbarously; I might even commit a murder and only be detained 'during the King's pleasure'. I could stand up in the market place and shout 'down with the police', and no one would mind. (As the Victorian policeman said about the anarchist who was making a speech against the Queen: 'It does 'er no 'arm and it does 'im a lot of good.') And yet, for all the appearance of freedom, the prison was escape-proof. I could choose whether I wanted to work in a factory or in an office (as I had before my RAF service); I could even set out as a tramp (no fun in October). But, wherever I went, the burglar-proof society would move smoothly on its infallible way, giving me nothing, allowing me to take nothing. I should have to work with it or starve. I felt a sudden irritable resentment against my parents for having no money to support me in the leisure to which I felt entitled.

At the Labour Exchange I sat on a bench with a line of unshaven men in raincoats, smelt the odour of wet clothes drying on the body, and tried to read my pocket copy of Marcus Aurelius. It struck me that it was all very well for him to be a philosopher; he was an emperor. But you couldn't be a philosopher if you had no money.

The man behind the counter asked me why I had left the RAF after six months. I said guiltily: 'Stomach trouble.' My discharge papers said 'Nervous unsuitability,' or something of the sort. But he didn't question me further; only asked what sort of work I wanted. The question seemed ironic; the correct reply was 'None.' That was human communication for you. So I said I thought I might like to try some kind of labouring job. He looked surprised. 'Not exactly the type, are you?' 'Still, it pays well,' I said, trying to look like a man with his head screwed on the right way. He flicked through a sheaf of cards, and finally selected one at random.

'How about this? Building site ten miles away. You've got to be outside here at seven in the morning.' I accepted the card, and went off to report to the foreman at the yard, which was within ten minutes' walk. He glanced at me from inside his wooden hut. 'Student?'

'No.'

'How long do you expect to stay?'

'Oh, a couple of months,' I said, trying to sound casual.

He tossed the card back at me. 'Post this back to the Exchange. Seven sharp in the morning. Bring sandwiches. There's no canteen.'

I felt better on the bus returning home; I was committed. A resignation descended on me. I still had thirty pounds left. I might be trapped, but at least I had a temporary breathing space, able to peer out from behind my wealth as if it was a fortification. My parents looked pleased when I told them about the job. There was beef stew for dinner (nobody in the Midlands calls the midday meal lunch), and it had steamed up the kitchen windows. My father's damp coat hung near the fire guard. (He always cycled to work, even in the snow.) The stone doors of the day closed on me like wings, enfolding and staining with an atmosphere I should always remember. I tried to throw off my depression as I gulped a basin of stew, and wondered what to do with the afternoon that lay between now and the end of freedom.

The job was not as bad as I had expected. I sat in the back of a canvas-covered lorry, bumping out towards Nottingham, while the blokes talked about the football results, and a youth of my own age talked about a piece of crumpet he'd had the night before, the daughter of his old headmaster, he claimed. No one took any notice of me. After five miles the cork popped out of my thermos flask and soaked my sandwiches with tea. I separated the damp sandwiches and threw them out, then wrapped the others in a sheet of the *Daily Mirror* that someone offered me. I looked automatically to see how many clothes Jane had taken off today. Someone mentioned that they had finished work at two o'clock the day before, because of the rain. I looked hopefully at the sky; but the sun had come out, reflected like steel in the puddles of water in the road.

The lorry stopped; we climbed down at a half-built factory in the middle of a field. Our job was to lay electric cables and dig trenches. I grabbed my pick awkwardly, like a schoolgirl who is unsure where to put her nose when she kisses. A friendly navvy immediately showed me the correct grip, and the way in which it should be swung for the best effect. He ended the short explanation with the words: 'It's a good navvy who can use a pick with his right or his left hand.' For some reason this advice stuck in my head as potentially valuable (although I've never found any use for it since). I was shown the spot where I had to dig, first loosening the stony earth with the pick, then shovelling it into a barrow and dumping it ten yards away. I began working like a madman in the chilly morning; in half-an-hour my RAF trousers were stained to the knees with clayey mud, and a piece of skin had come off my palm in an awkward place. 'Have to wank with your left hand now,' said the youth who had talked about the headmaster's daughter, and spat on his palms to show he was used to the work.

An hour later we stopped work, and sat in the canvas hut to eat our 'snap'. I was feeling depressed about the loss of my tea, but one of the navvies asked me if I would like to contribute half-a-dollar to the tea club; this would entitle me to three daily helpings of the tea brewed on the coke brazier outside the hut. I also discovered that, although our firm provided no canteen, a neighbouring firm who were in charge of concreting operations ran a small shop, housed in a wooden hut and run by a stringy, yellow-faced girl named Betty. She sold me some chocolate and four cream horns, which I ate with my tea; they immediately made me feel sick. But it had passed off two hours later, when I ate my sandwiches for dinner. So had the sunny weather; it was drizzling steadily, but no one brought up the subject of going home.

The foreman, a fat, toothless man named Skipper, suddenly took an interest in me and began to ask me questions. I turned them aside by asking *him* questions, and he began to tell me about the days when he had begun navvying, in the nineteen-twenties. 'Them wor the bad days,' he said. 'You lads dunno nothink about it. It's only them as lived through it can talk. Ain't that right, Tosh?' Tosh, an elderly man with skinny muscular arms, agreed, and began to talk about the means test, and of how he had once applied for National Assistance when he had been out of work for six months. The means test man had come to the house, and pointed out a set of fire irons, an empty coal bucket, and an armchair. 'You could get five bob for them in a junk shop. We can't give you money until you're destitute.' 'I'd have bashed the bleeder,' said the youth of wide sexual experience. 'You'd uv starved with the rest of us,' said the coddy, and chewed an immense chunk of cheese with his toothless gums.

We worked through the rain for another two hours, then helped to unload a drum of cable off a lorry. I was startled by an explosion and a flash like lightning that came from behind me. I turned and saw one of the men lying in a pool of water, an expression of astonishment on his face. He sat up and began to swear as the coddy came running over. I heard Tosh say: 'Trust Nipper. 'E's gone an put 'is bleeding pick through the cable.' I went over to look in the trench and saw the pick lying there, its blade discoloured as if by great heat. A lead-covered cable was almost invisible except at the point where the pick had severed it. 'You've never seen anythink like it,' said Nipper. 'This blue flame went up the pick an' in the air like a jet of water.' The electrician came over and told him he was lucky the handle of the pick was dry and he was wearing Wellington boots. 'You've sliced through twenty thousand volts.' Nipper looked rather pleased with himself, until the foreman began to swear at him and call him a careless bastard. Then we were all told to get back to our work, while the electrician began to patch up the cable. I was able to work close enough to watch him do this: he placed a two-foot-square rubber mat under the cable, squatted on it, and proceeded to chop at the cable with a hacksaw, handling the live end as casually as if it were a piece of rope.

The excitement brightened the day for me and made me feel suddenly at home on the building site. At three o'clock the rain began to pour down in such torrents that it made a white mist on the ground, and our trench was full of water in a matter of minutes. We rushed for the hut, and stood watching with a certain enthusiasm. We were soaked to the skin on a windy and chilly day, ten miles from the nearest town. And yet we were not working and we were being paid for working, and we all stood watching the rain and feeling happy. Finally the foreman summoned the lorry; we all piled into the back of it and went home. It was still raining heavily when we arrived back at the depot.

For about three days I observed the characters of the men minutely, determined to drain the last drop of experience from my self-imposed penance. At first they fascinated me. The most interesting character was a man called Terry, who joined us on the second day and took me under his wing. From the foreman's point of view he was about the worst possible tutor. He was expert at avoiding work, and taught me to do the same. He seemed to have an instinct that told him when to put on an appearance of industry, the times when the foreman was peering at us from behind a heap of rubble and earth. Otherwise he leaned on his shovel and smoked my cigarettes, and produced for me instalments of his life story, dating from the First World War.

He was a thin, brown-faced man, who had without exception the foulest mouth I have ever encountered. I tried to think of it as Rabelaisian, but there was an element of degradation in it that ruined the attempt. He split most of his infinitives, and many two-syllable nouns, with the same four-letter word. Every morning he met me with the same query — whether I had been 'on the nest' the night before. It was a purely rhetorical question, designed to make me ask him the same question, and lead the way to his own reminiscences. He had, apparently, an enormously fat wife, with whom he was always on bad terms. He had tried leaving her several times, but was too lazy to go far, and each time she had him arrested and put in jail for maintenance. He reckoned to spend a month of every year in our local jail. On Friday nights he invariably did a round of the pubs as soon as he had received his pay packet. Depending on how drunk he got, he might not bother to go home until Sunday, by which time he had no money left. But if he got home early enough on Friday (before midnight), he would poke his wife awake, demanding his marital privileges. 'Come on, ole girl, whadye think I pay yer for? Give us a bit,' and the pay packet would be handed over. But she always examined it first; he had once deceived her by stuffing it with torn squares of newspaper folded like notes. He also told me that his wife used to lock him out of the bedroom when he was very drunk, but had stopped doing that since he had developed a habit of sleeping with his teenage daughter. (I never discovered whether some of his unutterably foul stories of his sexual exploits — most of them unprintable — were invented by him or actually took place; if they were invented, he had the most fertile erotic imagination since de Sade.)

Terry had a fat friend of twenty-five or so named Peter, who possessed his foul mouth and ingenuity in splitting infinitives while lacking his redeeming vitality. There was really something awe-inspiring about Terry's salacious wit; he was not so much a fountain of obscenity as a combination of a sewage farm and an erupting volcano. The filth covered every area of human existence with complete impartiality. Peter was merely foul-mouthed and lazy. However, he was sacked after two days of leaning on his shovel, and Terry adopted me instead. (I noticed the dark looks the foreman gave me, but what could I do without hurting Terry's feelings?)

I stuck the job for three weeks. Then the icy weather set in, and we worked hard to keep warm. The erotically inclined youth whom I had met on my first day also got into the habit of trying to work near me, and telling me stories of his conquests that I knew to be

13

lies. He had been in approved schools twice (for six months each time), and was the most futile bore I have ever met. He referred to all girls as 'tarts', and was not afraid to enter into details of sadistic and fetishistic fantasies which most men would reserve for the psychiatrist's couch or the confessional. He mistook my politeness for respect, and lost no opportunity of sharing the same wheelbarrow with me so that he could allow his mind to buzz in slow, repetitive circles over the same area of perverse wish-fulfilment. His pale eyes and pale hair and slack mouth have since come to assume a symbolic status for me; whenever I read in a newspaper of some sexual murder, I think of him as the killer, without willpower or sense of his own identity, easily influenced by a television advertisement or a casual word, yet with his mind incredibly concentrated upon the only subject that interested him.

After a few days, my interest in the navvies as individuals disappeared; all my impressions merged in a sense of futility. I was one of them; I even caught myself speculating on how many years I should have to work before I could be a foreman. I was bored. But my tendency to accept the pattern of my everyday life as inevitable — the same tendency that made me accept the first job I was offered — made me continue to get up at six-fifteen every morning and catch the first bus (six-forty) into the centre of town. In the evenings I read or listened to concerts on the radio.

We finished working at the half-built factory and moved into town, digging up a cobbled street to relay cables that had been there for the past fifty years. I was able to get up later and go home earlier. One day an old navvy took me aside to give me a lecture: 'Get out of this job. You're not intended for it. A navvy's the lowest of the low. Once you're a navvy, you're good for nothing else. I've been in it for thirty years, and I wish't I had sense to get out of it sooner. Nobody else wants you when you've been a navvy. It's worse than jail....' Even this warning had no effect. I was settled into the hypnotic routine of physical work. In the eyes of the gods who organise our lives, navvying is a 'reserved occupation'; no moral or intellectual demands are made on the labourer; he is allowed to ignore the problem of the meaning of human life. I drifted happily, completely identified with the lot of the working man — that is to say, with Terry and Tosh and Nipper and Sammy (the oversexed youth) and the rest.

It took the death of my grandfather to winkle me out of my home town and the shell of democratic tolerance I had accepted. I was lying in bed on a Saturday morning when my mother came into the room and said simply: 'Your grandad's dead.' She did not seem upset, neither did I expect her to be. Half-an-hour later, when I had rubbed the sleep out of my eyes, I went down to breakfast — an egg and bacon that had lost their freshness after being left on the hob to warm. My mother was sweeping the floor and listening to Music While You Work. My grandfather had not seemed very ill; he had been confined to his bed on several odd occasions over the past year, but the doctor was not alarmed. I had meant to go and see him on the previous evening, but had taken my younger brother to a concert at the local working men's club instead. His heart had stopped in the night. I finished the egg with a piece of dip, and asked my mother: 'Do you feel upset?'

'No. It had to happen some time, didn't it?'

I am sure she was fond of her father, but being upset about his death would have struck her as pointless.

After breakfast I went to my grandmother's to see if I could do anything. Several members of the family were sitting there, drinking tea and commiserating.

My grandmother seemed a little dazed. Family gatherings bored me, so I went off on the pretext of registering the death; the registrar closed at midday on Saturday, so I had to hurry. On the bus up town I tried to think about the death. I had only ever had one grandfather; the other had been killed in the first war. Grandad had spoilt me from the beginning. I was the first grandchild born into the family, and my grandparents never cared for the later arrivals as much as for me. Besides — there's no point in being modest about this — my cousins were a dull lot, shy and awkward. Not having been petted from birth, as I was, perhaps they lacked the self-confidence that comes from taking one's luck for granted. I am not sure whether I loved my grandparents, but I took their love as a matter of course. My grandmother was the gentlest and most inoffensive woman I have ever known; my grandfather was a cheerful man with red hair, inclined to get drunk and offer to fight the pub. My grandmother worshipped him. I found him a pleasant man, who bought me sweets and told me dirty jokes from the time I was five years old. (I hasten to add that their humour was always coprological, never sexual.)

So I went up town on the bus and thought about him, and realised that I did not care about his death any more than if he had gone away for a week to visit relatives in Durham. I found this hard to understand. Was I a heartless grandson? Had I not received gifts from him throughout my life, from a chemistry set and incendiary bomb powder (this when he was in the ARP during the war) to a bicycle — which he had rashly promised to give me at the end of the war, obviously believing that it would go on for ever?

So I took in his death certificate, had two pints in the pub over the road, and went home. And on the following Wednesday I took the day off to attend the funeral.

At the last minute I decided not to go to the graveside; instead, I waited in my grandmother's house until they all came back. They opened a bottle of sherry and produced sandwiches and biscuits, and we all sat around talking cheerfully. Then, suddenly, my grandmother burst into loud wails, and rushed out of the room. One of my uncles went with her. I heard him assuring her that grandad was in a better place, but she went on crying.

I stared across at the picture on the wall — of myself at two years of age, sitting on grandad's shoulders. Then the answer fell into place, like the final word that completes a crossword puzzle. I was not upset by his death because I did not believe in it. Death was illogical. Either he was not dead, or he had never been alive. But the world was still the same; everything went on. You could not convince me that something had *happened*. I sat there and thought: That's it. *Things don't happen!* If they happened, the world would need a complete reassessment. But, as human beings, we proceed on the assumption that things won't happen. That is why I might have stayed in the navvying job for twenty years and become a foreman; that is why people get up every morning and go off to work and marry girls who seem attractive and make the best of them for the rest of their lives. The world slides on, easily and silently; there is nothing to get excited about because there is nothing to be gained and nothing lost. Whatever is real has nothing to do with this world where things don't happen. And nothing matters.

As I thought of this I watched my uncle Ernie carving a slice off the huge ham on the table, and a feeling of joy made me bodiless. I felt like getting up and poking the pictures and the tablecloth like a doctor examining an interesting case, and saying: 'How curious. What an extraordinary world. Yes, really most interesting. I haven't seen a world like this one before. I must make a note of it.' It was such a pure detachment that I wanted to leave immediately, to try it, like a new pair of glasses, on the outside world. So I got up and slipped out, as if to go to the lavatory, murmuring to my mother, 'See you at home,' and went through the garden gate. The world had grown light, almost weightless. I could lift it and do what I liked with it. It was no longer simply 'there', meaningless or incomprehensible. Consequently, I had better start putting it to some use. I felt patronising about people as I passed them in the street; I wanted to nod at them reassuringly, and smile as if to say: 'Don't worry, I know the world seems pretty nasty and serious. But it's all right. I'm in control now.'

It was impossible to go back to work, even for a day. I rang the office of the building firm from a call-box, and invented some story about having to go to London immediately to clear up some of my grandfather's business. I had to leave at eleven in the morning. Could I dispense with notice, and have my wages sent on to my home when they were ready? They were quite amiable; men come and go in the building trade; a day's notice is usually enough. They obviously believed I had found another job, for they asked me if I wanted to call in for my cards that afternoon. I said no; I didn't think I should be needing my cards for some time to come.

As I left the call-box, the sun broke through the November mist. I remembered grandad, and suddenly felt a real and deep affection born of gratitude. He had always given me things; his death was a kind of last gift to me.

The next morning I gave my mother five pounds and took a train to London, carrying a cardboard suitcase and a haversack full of books. The world had regained its normal weight, but my course was altered; I had been switched on to another railway line.

Part 1

Chapter One

I ARRIVED AT St. Pancras in the late afternoon, and immediately made my way to the Youth Hostel in Great Ormond Street. This was the third time I had been in London; the two previous occasions had been during my RAF service, and had lasted a day each. I handed over my card, wrote 'hiker' in the book, and dumped my bags in the dormitory. I was wearing a dyed RAF overcoat over old corduroy trousers and a woollen sweater.

As I went into the tube at Russell Square I felt out of place among the crowd of neatly dressed clerks and girls who looked like models. I fell into a gloomy and defensive frame of mind. I travelled to Leicester Square, walked up the Charing Cross Road (the book-shops were just closing, to my disgust), and finally found a cheap café in Tottenham Court Road, where I got egg and chips for one-and-sixpence. I was disappointed in my fellow customers. I expected them to look like out-of-work writers or actors, but they looked more like spivs and racing touts. I took care, when paying for my meal, to hold my wallet under the table while I extracted a pound note; I didn't want to risk somebody spotting the wad of notes. I glanced through a copy of the *Star* that someone had left behind, and learned that James Dean had died in a car crash, and that his fans all over the States were mourning his death. I felt a certain satisfaction about this, for although I knew nothing about Dean it seemed to me that one film actor less in the world could only be a good thing, a step in the right direction. If a far-sighted destiny would arrange enough accidents of this sort, the world might be left in the hands of really intelligent people, and thus be nearer the millennium. If you live in a world that bores you, any sort of violent accident seems a change for the better, and a newspaper headline announcing the death of a politician or the discovery of another mass-murderer in Austria produces a pleasant sensation of movement.

Brooding in this manner, I made my way down the Charing Cross Road, and stopped at a pub on the corner of Old Compton Street. I had eaten too much to drink beer, so I had a whisky; since I was unused to spirits, it produced an immediate exhilaration. After a few minutes a bearded youth came in with an arty-looking girl; she wore thick red stockings and a duffle coat. I tried smiling at her when she glanced in my direction, but she looked away as if I were invisible. This annoyed me, and I realised why I felt so rebellious about London. The whole city was a part of the great unconscious conspiracy of matter to make you feel non-existent. It produced in me the opposite of the feeling of weightlessness which I had had at the funeral. A city can sit gently on you and squash you flat. It is a monument to your unimportance, a perpetual gesture of disrespect from the universe to people who lack a sense of their own necessity. I had been reading a gloomy novel by Pisemsky called *A Thousand Souls* in which a young idealist marries for money and betrays everyone he loves. Abruptly I understood the meaning of the book. If a devil had appeared beside me and offered to make me complete master of London, on condition that I renounced every other ambition, I think I might have accepted. Unfortunately there was no devil to tempt me; nobody cared that much.

So I wandered back to Great Ormond Street, exhausted and depressed, using a half-crown street atlas to navigate my way, and wishing that some adventure would happen to me. But nothing did, and I arrived back at the hostel at eight o'clock and found a crowd of hearties in cross-country kit singing puerile songs about the difficulty of getting to heaven in a rocking chair and ten green bottles hanging on a wall. There was a copy of *The Memoirs of Sherlock Holmes* in the hostel library (I felt morally unfitted to read any of the philosophical volumes I had brought with me), and I took it up to the dormitory, where I read until ten o'clock. I found it difficult to believe that Conan Doyle's London and mine were the same place. I fell asleep long after the hearties had come to bed, wondering where I should start looking for a cheap room, and what kind of work I should do. I was determined not to spend another night in the hostel if it could be avoided. The next morning, after sweeping out the dining-hall and paying my one-and-sixpence, I collected my hostel card and walked down Southampton Row in search of breakfast. I bought a copy of the *London Weekly Advertiser,* and settled down to study it in a coffee bar, while I ate a cheese sandwich. There seemed to be a great many advertisements for rooms to let; I marked half-a-dozen in pencil, asked the girl behind the counter for some pennies, and went out to a call-box. The London telephones baffled me; I had never before seen telephones with letters as well as numbers on the dial. So I tried dialling the operator and asking for the number I wanted. This method worked well enough, but the operator took an unconscionably long time to reply. The first two numbers I rang had already let their rooms (these were the cheapest, at twenty-five shillings each). The third — a woman with a foreign voice — asked me what work I did, and when I replied that I was a student she said she wanted a working man who would be out all day and hung up on me. I was beginning to feel discouraged. I dialled the operator again, waited a quarter-of-an-hour or so until she replied, and asked for another number. She asked me

23

irritably why I couldn't dial it, and then explained impatiently how I could do so. This cheered me up; I had already been in the box for half-an-hour, and two people were striding up and down outside and periodically glaring at me. Always susceptible to public opinion, I decided to make this my last call. But the man who replied told me the landlady was out, and could I ring back in half-an-hour? So I gave up the box. A little woman swept past me, muttering, 'About time, too,' and I sat on a nearby wall to wait my turn again. Already London was beginning to seem one of the most detestable cities I had ever been in. Ten minutes later it began to rain, and the little woman was still talking busily, now smiling and laughing with animation, and sometimes making gestures with her hands, as if to say, 'Would you believe it?' A man in a raincoat strode up and down and glared in through the glass; finally he grew annoyed, and tried tapping on the glass with a coin. The door flew open; the woman, her gloved hand over the mouthpiece, shouted: 'DO you mind!' and slammed the door again. The man glared at me venomously, as if I were to blame for all this. I decided to go and look for another call-box; besides, the rain was now falling in a sheet. I hurried on for fifty yards, and found myself outside Holborn underground station. I walked inside and stared at the tube map, trying to find a name I recognised. There was Kentish Town and Whitechapel and Earls Court. In my early teens I had been a student of murder, and all these places aroused memories of violence. I seemed to remember the murder of a prostitute in a cheap room off the Earls Court Road. If cheap rooms were available there, the district was worth investigating. So I took a ticket to Earls Court. In the train I scanned my *Advertiser*. Sure enough, I found two addresses in Earls Court; I located these in my street atlas before I got off the train.

The first proved to be a little overawing. It was a large house that stood among other identical large houses in a tree-shaded square. At first I wondered if there could be some mistake; the place looked more like the town house of one of Oscar Wilde's characters. But the address in the advertisement was clear enough, so I rang the doorbell. A coloured maid opened it; when I said I was looking for a room she nodded pleasantly, and led me up four flights of stairs. The carpets were thick and red, and the wall decorations were of a kind I had only seen in Hollywood musicals. I had a premonition that I was about to be shown a fifteen-guinea-a-week flat and that I should feel very foolish explaining that I was looking for something about ten times as cheap. But she led me up a final narrow flight of stairs (with no carpet, only linoleum), and showed me a tiny room with a gas-fire, a single bed, an armchair and a table. It was icy cold.

I glanced out of the window at roofs and back gardens, and asked diffidently how much it was. She said she would have to ask the landlady. She led me back to the first floor, where she rang the bell of an enormous white door with a cut glass knob. After a long delay a tall woman in a dressing-gown opened it. She had a beaky nose and the eyes of a bird, and she ignored me, rasping at the maid: 'Well, Matilda?' like a headmistress demanding an explanation.

'This gen'lman'd lahk a room, ma'am.'

The sharp eyes now turned on me; I felt she should have held a lorgnette to stare at me through. 'Which one? The top one?'

'The one you advertised,' I explained.

'I have no idea which we advertised,' she said acidly. 'I leave all that to my agent.'

'The top one, ma'am,' Matilda said.

'It's two pounds fifteen a week,' the woman said, surveying me as if to say, 'I am sure this person can't afford it.'

By this time I felt so thoroughly in the wrong that I put on an overjoyed expression, as if such cheapness surpassed all my hopes, and said: 'Good. I'd like to take it.'

'Can you pay a week in advance?'

'Certainly,' I said, fumbling for my wallet.

She made a little aggrieved motion, and raised her eyebrows at me. 'Give it to Matilda,' she said, and closed the door on us.

Matilda grinned at me sympathetically, and led me back upstairs. She showed me the location of the bathroom and lavatory, how to put shillings in the gas meter, and how to light the gas fire without causing an explosion. Finally she went off with three pounds, and returned with five shillings change and a front door key. Then I was left alone in my own room at last. The warmth from the gas-fire had given it a smell of hot linoleum. I arranged my few books at the back of the table, threw my clothes into a drawer, and lay down on the bed. The rent seemed absurdly expensive — most of the single rooms in the *Advertiser* ranged from twenty-five to thirty-five shillings — but, after all, I could find somewhere cheaper at my leisure.

I decided to wash my hands, and then go out and buy some food. I made my way down to the bathroom, but the door proved to be locked. I tried one on the floor below, but that was locked too. Finally I met my landlady, still floating around in her quilted satin dressing-gown. She stared at me coldly, and asked me if I was looking for something. I told her the bathrooms were locked.

'But of course they're locked. They're always locked in the mornings, after nine o'clock. If you want a bath,

26

you have to pay a shilling for it. I found that dishonest people were sneaking in during the day to avoid paying.' Her stare showed me that she felt I was quite capable of this. She added: 'If you want to wash your hands, you'll find a wash-bowl in most of the lavatories.' As I tried to sneak off, she called me back. 'Hasn't Matilda told you about the rules?'

'No.'

'Then I'd better. There's no cooking in the rooms or any kind of perishable food allowed. The gas ring is for making tea only. If I catch any of my lodgers cooking food, I reserve the right to give them half-an-hour's notice. Is that clear?' She ticked off the points on her fingers. 'I don't allow visitors in the house after ten o'clock. I don't like lights left on in the rooms when there's no one in them. Our electricity bills are enormous. It's no trouble to switch off a light if you go downstairs to the lavatory. And finally, I don't allow women in the men's rooms or vice versa. This house has a good reputation.' She began to walk away, dismissing me, then turned back again as I started up the stairs. 'One more thing. You'll notice there are negro tenants in the house. Some landladies won't have them, but I don't hold these prejudices. But I think the white people in the house should try to set them an example of good manners and tidiness. They can easily be taught with a little patience. They don't understand our ways yet. We ought to try and help them. So if you notice any of the black tenants breaking the house rules, I hope you'll remember to mention it to me.'

This time she allowed me to go. I washed my hands and face, went into a cold sweat when I discovered that I'd left my light on while I was out of the room, and scuttled out of the house. I wandered along Earls Court Road in the thin drizzle, and stared morosely at the crowds that made walking along the pavement a feat of navigation. The sight of a second-hand bookshop cheered me, and I spent a quarter-of-an-hour browsing through its shelves. I might have spent longer, but the uncertain condition of my stomach caused a constant disturbance in my intestines and bowels, and I moved surrounded by an odour of vegetable decay. This is a subject not usually mentioned by novelists; yet it plays its small but distinct part in our everyday lives. (Even those advertisements that speak so frankly of body-odour and bad breath have not yet thought of suggesting tablets that will deodorise the fetor of the bowels, or disguise it under some more acceptable perfume.) So I bought a copy of a translation of some plays by Grillparzer, and a volume of stories by Andreyev, and wandered out into the rain, feeling pleased with myself.

Finally I found an ABC, where I drank three cups of coffee and stared out into the wet street, the Grillparzer open in front of me. *Der Traum, Ein Leben;* I had been familiar with the play since I was fourteen; after Flecker's *Hassan* it was my favourite play. A dream, a life. But the words were meaningless as I sat in a café on a wet Friday morning. It would be intensely comforting if life were a dream or a night-mare. Unfortunately, it is neither. This London was no 'unreal city', *fourmillante cité, cité pleine de rêves,* ten-anted by ghosts. It was tenanted by landladies like the one I had just left behind in Courtfield Gardens, and women like the one who had pushed past me into the phone-box; people too busy to care much about one another; people who had to push their way through crowds into jammed trains, to queue for meals in crowded ABCs or struggle through a packed self-service grocery store. Suddenly it all seemed horrible and absurd. This was not civilization. Why did people live in this city? To distract myself, I read the introduction to the volume of Andreyev's stories. From this I learned that Andreyev considered life completely futile, that most of his stories deal with the ways in which people deceive themselves, and how, when the illusions disappear, they are left with nothing but 'the basic pain of existence'. My natural optimism tended to reject this extreme view. On the other hand, when I looked out of the window to consider an alternative, I found myself staring at a hoarding which advertised a series on Christian faith by a well-known writer for women's magazines. His face, boyish and confiding, but twenty times larger than life, stared across the road at me, urging on me the necessity of buying a certain Sunday newspaper to read about his new Pilgrim's Progress. I finished my coffee and went out.

Back in my room, I counted my money — it still amounted to about twenty pounds — and tried to work out on a notepad how long I could make it last me. Of one thing I was certain — I felt no immediate desire to look for work. The more I saw of London, the more I thought nostalgically about retiring to some ivy-covered old tower in the country, like a character in a Peacock novel, and spending my days studying the Church Fathers. The alternative was to find the local Labour Exchange and ask for some well-paid labouring job, or a job in an office. Of course, there *must* be jobs that I should enjoy doing, somewhere in London. In a theatre, for example, or a publisher's office. But my ignorance was so complete that I could only hope for the benevolence of fate to guide me towards them. And I had an instinct which told me that fate had no intention of serving me well. A destiny that could guide me to the house in Courtfield Gardens was obviously looking forward to playing further jokes on me.

I sat staring out of the window, aware of all kinds of feelings that I could not resolve. There was resentment, but resentment towards what? Society? An abstraction. Destiny? Probably a superstition. The problem was simpler than that. In spite of the difficulties and miseries, I liked being alive. In fact, there were times when I became aware of life as a terrifying power capable of turning men into gods. But the world was arranged in such a way that I could never get to grips with that kind of power. I was still smarting with resentment about my landlady. Why did such people exist? Why did she want to browbeat fellow human beings? It would be a very satisfying world in which her kind could be struck dead by the loathing they aroused. Suddenly my bewilderment crystallised into a fierce detestation of the woman and the world she represented. I knew with certainty what I wanted and what I hated. It suddenly seemed that all civilisation had been a false start, a complication that hid the realities. The reality was simple: power, the overwhelming violence of history. But the condition of living in society was a ritual that left no time for contemplation of the power. Life had to be more simple; I had to learn to simplify it... I thought nostalgically of Rousseau's idea of living in trees, and of the advantage possessed by Hindu ascetics in their temperate climate.

***

I decided that the best way to conserve money would be to stay in my room as much as possible. So in the afternoon I walked up to the Kensington Public Library and spent a couple of quiet hours wandering around there. But towards five o'clock, when I left the library, the sight of the crowds in the lighted streets disturbed me, and I walked along in the direction of Hyde Park. It was a cold evening with a slight mist. My hours in the library had calmed me; I was in a mood to absorb the colour and light around me. I realised I was glad to be in London. The city might be irritating and exhausting, yet there was an exhilaration in floating in its bloodstream. Even the Albert Memorial struck me as curiously exciting. (I remembered the story about Harry Thaw, the murderer of the architect Stanford White; when he saw the Albert Memorial he is reputed to have said: 'My god, I shot the wrong bloody architect.') Beecham was presenting a series of concerts at the Albert Hall. Count Basie was bringing his band to the newly built Festival Hall. I passed the Knightsbridge Barracks, where a debutante had recently been caught at midnight in a barrack-room of guardsmen. A woman in furs came out of the Hyde Park Hotel screaming 'Texi!' It was all unresolvable, as it had been a few hours earlier, but this no longer worried me. The towers of Babylon might have been as unreal and as bright. I felt a sensation that puzzled and startled me. It was love: not love for London or for people; a love that was bodiless and disconnected, without an object, love like brandy on a cold night.

I took a bus from Knightsbridge to Cambridge Circus, tired of walking. I paused for a while on the corner of Shaftesbury Avenue to watch two buskers singing to the music of an accordion, then went into the pub I had sat in the night before. It was still almost empty. I took my half-pint of bitter into a corner, and began to read my Andreyev. But I had no concentration. I kept thinking that if I sat there another half-hour there would be nothing more to do except go to another pub, or take a bus back home. Or I might queue for a seat in the gods of some theatre. They were showing Eliot's *Confidential Clerk* somewhere. Every time the door opened I found myself looking up, as if expecting a friend.

For some reason I stayed long after half-an-hour, and drank a second half of bitter. I have wondered since if some instinct told me to expect new events in my life. I sat there for no reason I could understand, and then the door opened and a rather beautiful girl of twenty or so came in alone. She bought herself a sherry, then stood uncertainly at the bar, glancing round the room. No one paid any attention to her, although she would have created a sensation in any pub in my home town. The seat next to mine was one of the few in the room that was still empty. I suppose I looked harmless enough, reading my book. She came over and sat down next to me. I went on reading, slightly disturbed by her perfume. She lit a cigarette. After a few moments she said: 'Excuse me, is this the only public bar, or is there another one through there?'

I'm not sure,' I said, eager to be of service. 'I could easily find out.'

At this moment someone bent over us and asked me: 'Like me to make a sketch of your lady friend for you?'

I glanced from the girl to the man, bewildered for a moment, then said: 'I'm afraid we're not together.'

'My apologies,' the man said smoothly. He had an extremely pleasant voice that drawled slightly, an actor's voice. He was carrying a large folder and a sketch pad. He was wearing a plaid thing over his shoulders that might have been a cloak or an overcoat.

The girl took the opportunity to ask him: 'Do you happen to know if there's another bar through there?'

'There is.'

'In that case, I'd better go and look in there. I'm waiting for someone.'

She got up, leaving her sherry on the table, and went out. The artist sat down opposite me.

'They're always waiting for someone,' he said conversationally. I said I was afraid so. He confided: 'Thought she was one of these American tourists, from the look of her.' At this moment the girl came back. (I think we were both surprised to see her again.) She said: 'He's not in there either,' and sat down again. The artist immediately leaned forward, his face radiating a curious mixture of intimacy and respect, and said: 'In that case, there's time for me to sketch you. I charge half-a-crown for my portraits, but if you don't like it, you needn't have it.'

'All right,' the girl said. 'But if he comes in while you're doing it I shall have to go.'

'Lucky man,' the artist sighed.

I glanced up and caught the eye of the barman, who was staring across at us with an air of definite disfavour. I realised that the artist was sitting without a drink, so I asked him if I could buy him one.

'That's extremely decent of you, old boy. I'll take a half of bitter.'

I bought the beer, placed it in front of him, then sat down again and watched him as he sketched the girl. I was feeling rather pleased with myself. It was a human contact, at least. I was sitting with a girl I had never seen before and a man I had never seen before, and there was a cobweb of intimacy between the three of us. I looked at the girl's profile as she asked: 'Do you do this for a living?'

'No. I'm an actor... when I have work.'

'I thought so, somehow.'

From where I was sitting I could watch the progress of the sketch. It was not a very good likeness, and the ball-pen he was using did nothing to improve it. I reminded myself to use charcoal if I ever tried this; with judicious rubbing, charcoal sketches can always be made to look impressive. I studied the artist as he worked. It was somehow not difficult to tell that he was an actor. The face was handsome in a dark-brown sort of way; he had the good looks of a *jeune premier*. The clothes he wore were not particularly new, but they were well-cut: a dark suit, a tartan shirt and a yellow cravat. On closer inspection, I could see that the object he wore round his shoulders was an overcoat, worn like a cloak with sleeves folded in. His hair was dark and wavy — in the manner of a matinée idol, or an advertisement for hair oil.

While he worked, he asked her casually: 'With your delightful accent I guess you're not a Londoner?'

'No, from New Zealand.'

'Have you visited this bootleg den before?'

'No. I don't like going into pubs on my own.'

'But you tossed your scruples aside on this occasion.'

'I'm waiting for someone to take me to the theatre.'

'Is he late?'

'A little.' She looked anxious.

'What will you do if he doesn't turn up?'

'I... I don't know. Go home.'

'At short notice! Can't you ring him?'

'No... I don't know his telephone number.'

'Ah.' He glanced up over the sketch, considered her for a moment, then asked: 'New acquaintance?'

She looked undecided whether to resent it or be candid. She said finally: 'I met him last night.'

'In a pub?'

'No. Why do you ask?'

'I feel a kind of duty towards New Zealanders. My best friend in the army came from Christchurch. I almost married his sister, as a matter of fact. So I always like talking to New Zealanders. They're so innocent. You're innocent, for example. Otherwise, why are you talking to two strange men in a Soho pub?'

I felt flattered at being included, although I realised

that it was probably his way of reassuring her — safety in numbers, and so on. The girl seemed to be quite won over by his explanation; she even told us her name — Doreen Taylor. I introduced myself at this point. Finally, the artist told us his name — James Street. His full name, he said, was James Compton Street, but people in Soho thought this was a bad joke. (This had to be explained to the girl, who had never heard of Old Compton Street.) James finished his sketch and showed it to her. I watched her face closely, but she showed no sign of disappointment. 'I like it,' she said. 'Isn't it rather a flattering likeness?'

'Flattery is the sincerest form of imitation,' James said. Then, as she opened her handbag, 'No, wait. Let me make a suggestion. It looks as if your friend doesn't intend to turn up. So why don't you use the half-crown to buy us three coffees round the corner? Then I could show you Soho properly.'

The idea obviously appealed to her, but she was uncertain.

'I ought to give him another five minutes.'

The idea of spending the rest of the evening in her company was so delightful that I joined forces with James to dissuade her from waiting another minute. James began to talk persuasively about his qualifications as a guide to Soho. Finally she stood up. 'I suppose he won't come now anyway. We might as well go.' As she spoke the door opened and a flashily dressed youth came in; he wore a bright check overcoat and an American style hat. He waved to her from across the room.

I heard James mutter: 'Damn and blast'.

'Here he is,' the girl said.

James leaned over and said quickly: 'Can you be in here the same time tomorrow? I'll complete the sketch then.' By this time her escort had crossed the room to us. But she nodded very quickly as he came up. I noted the almost feline look of self-satisfaction that spread over James's face for a second.

Doreen introduced us to the man, whose name I have now forgotten. He had a brick-red face and spoke with a Cockney accent. Even with my inexperience I should have guessed him to be connected with racing. His apologies were brief: 'Sorry I'm late, lav. Got 'eld up with some of the boys.' He regarded us with mistrust.

'Two old friends of mine,' Doreen said. Luckily, she had our names off pat.

The Cockney said gruffly: 'Pleased ter know yer', then took her arm. 'Cam on. We'd better get crackin' if we don't want to be late.' He hauled her off unceremoniously.

James called: 'See you soon, Doreen', and got a quick smile in reply. I felt a flash of triumph (although it was no advantage to me that he had persuaded her to meet him the next day).

Then they went, and James sat down again and emptied his half-pint, saying: 'Mmm, pity. We almost made it. Still, there's always another day. What did you think of her?'

'Wonderful!' I said with sincerity.

'Looks loaded, don't you think?'

'Loaded?'

'With money. Probably a rich tourist.'

I was slightly shocked by this attitude. 'But surely you're not interested in whether she has money or not?'

He looked at me with slightly raised eyebrows.

'No. I wouldn't mind her in my bed, with or without money. Still, the money forms... how shall we say, an additional attraction.' I decided that he was trying to shock me, and determined not to be shocked. 'Will you have another drink?'

'Mmm, I don't know. I shouldn't drink any more until I've eaten. I haven't had a meal today yet.'

'Do you intend to eat now?'

'I *would* have eaten — if Doreen had paid up her half-crown. As it is, I shall have to find another customer first.'

I glanced over at the barman, who was still keeping a cautious eye on us.

'I don't think the man behind the bar wants us to stay around. He keeps staring at us.'

'I know. He doesn't like me. Perhaps I'll find another pub. Want to come?'

'Couldn't I persuade you to have a meal with me first?'

I found myself uttering the words with no kind of forethought. He was broke; it seemed the most natural thing in the world to offer to buy him a meal.

'That's very civilised of you. It'll be a pleasure. I always work better on a full stomach.'

'I know a café just up the road,' I said, thinking of the place I had been to on the previous evening.

'That's no good,' he said, without bothering to find out which one I meant. 'I'll take you to a good place.'

So we went out into the Charing Cross Road, and walked along towards Dean Street. I felt a certain misgiving. His 'good place' might be more expensive than I anticipated. His remark about the girl having money came back to me. For a moment I wondered if I had fallen into the hands of one of those smooth confidence tricksters who are supposed to abound in Soho; I decided not to let him know how much money I had on me. Five minutes later, I felt ashamed of my suspicions; we were in a dingy basement near Shaftesbury Avenue, surrounded by Greek voices and a smell I later learned to be Greek cooking. The walls were painted an unappetising green, and ran with moisture. The tabletops were covered with oilcloth. In the next room several men played billiards and bar-football. A fat man passed the menu from behind the tea urn — he seemed to know James — and we studied it together. It seemed, if anything, cheaper than the place I had been in the night before. We ordered kebab and chips, and two cups of tea arrived immediately, together with a plate of chunky bread and butter.

James proceeded to cross-examine me. When I spoke of the compulsion to leave my home town, he nodded sympathetically.

'I once played there in panto. Filthy dump. Richest town in the Midlands, and they won't even run a decent theatre.' He went off into a reminiscence about a woman he'd had an affair with, the wife of a business man whom I knew by sight. Her influence had kept him at work in the town for several months. 'Trouble was, she almost wore me out. She was an absolute monster. Still, blaggers can't be choosers.'

To divert him from this melancholy train of thought, I asked him what a man of his obvious talent was doing sketching in pubs at half-a-crown a time. He said with quick interest: 'How do you know I have talent?'

'You have a good voice and an imposing manner. Surely you could find work — if only in some provincial company?'

He expanded like a spring day, and stroked his chin with a manner that reminded me of Sir Jasper in pantomime.

'No doubt I could, but who wants to work in the provinces? The theatre's dying. I'd rather stay in London and wait for the West End to recognise me.'

'Why don't you try auditioning?'

'I prefer to live as I am. I don't like chasing things — except, of course, women. Even there, I have no spirit of competition. If a girl seems eager, I'm happy to oblige.'

The food arrived; a dark-skinned girl brought it, and smiled at James. Her accent was delightful.

'And how iss the great actor today?'

James placed his hand lightly on his breast.

'Very well, thank you, my dear. And you?'

'Good.'

He took her hand and began examining it. 'I see you've been manicuring your nails again. Been fighting with your husband?' He explained to me: 'She gets his skin under her nails.'

Something in his manner brought back memories that I found elusive. When he talked to the girl his voice became smooth, slightly purring, and deeper than usual. His eyes seemed to retreat slightly, as if regarding her from some depth of detachment and subjectivity. His manner was like a caress. Then it came to me: it was a sort of mixture of Rudolph Valentino in *The Sheik* and Charles Boyer in *The Constant Nymph*. There was something curiously stylised about it, like making a deep bow and scraping the foot. I came later to christen this James's Great Lover Manner. To my surprise, girls seem pleased and flattered by it rather than hypnotised. But then, my knowledge of feminine psychology is nil.

When the Greek girl had gone, James said: 'Lovely piece of charver, that.'

'Charver?'

'Ahem, quite. My own coinage. The Anglo-Saxon word is short and lacking in euphony. I borrowed it from the Russian. It means glory or homage. Surely appropriate?'

He began singing the opening chorus of *Prince Igor:*

'Charver, charver, knyazu charver, char — ar-ver!'

'Surely the word is "slava"?' I suggested.

He looked impressed.

'You are a scholar. Still, it doesn't make any difference. In fact, now you mention it, I believe charver is a

Polynesian word meaning "that which surpasseth understanding".'

We ate the meal and then went to another local pub, where James persuaded a tipsy business man and a courting couple to allow him to sketch them. He insisted on buying me a whisky. When I pointed out that he would need the money, he made a characteristic sweeping gesture with his left hand *(The Desert Song* — the Red Shadow summons his warriors to battle), and said: 'Pooh, I have eaten today.'

Even at this early stage my attitude to James was ambivalent. I was flattered that he should consider me worthy of his acquaintance; I felt a certain Doctor Watson-ish admiration for the charm and confidence of his manner. (At nineteen, I was miserably aware of my own uncertainty.) Yet I was also amused by his stylised panache; and here my admiration was directed not so much at his mastery of the sweeping manner as at his audacity in managing to get away with such old-fashioned stuff. He seemed to be the most confident, the least self-divided man I had ever met. And yet I felt no envy, for in a subtle way he flattered me; the freedom from self-division had been achieved at a price I was not willing to pay. My curiosity about him was limitless, being a painless form of self-analysis.

Half-an-hour before closing time a crowd of art students came in. James left me sitting in a corner, staring muzzily at the dart-board (I was floating somewhere near the ceiling), and went over to speak to them. I am still not sure whether he knew them, or whether he simply wanted to sketch them. Five minutes later he joined me outside in the gents. 'Delightful little girl I've just met. Do you know anything about Russian literature?'

'A bit. Why?'

'Come and engage her boyfriend in conversation.

He's doing a thesis on Russian writers.'

I remember staring around amiably at a crowd of faces that occasionally blurred, and being introduced by James as 'my friend Harry' (I am sure he had forgotten my other name). When James introduced me to a girl named Myra, he found the opportunity to wink at me. She was short and plump, with a long nose; she wore a black duffel coat. I found her pink cheeks attractive. Her boyfriend was a pale youth with a blond beard, who immediately began to talk to me about Dostoevsky. (I discovered that James had introduced me as the author of a book on Dostoevsky's early works.) Glowing with confidence — the result of six pints of beer — I talked expansively about Aksakov and Pisemsky. (As I suspected, he had not read either.) At some point in the conversation James disappeared with Myra, but the bearded youth seemed uninterested; he went on describing his theory that Dostoevsky had murdered his father and been in love with his mother. The bell rang for closing time; I bought a final round, changing yet another pound note. Then we all trooped outside; we exchanged goodnights, and I found myself alone. I walked with a rolling gait in the direction of Oxford Street. (I was not completely drunk, but I enjoyed pretending I was.) At the corner of Rathbone Place someone grabbed my arm. It was James, who was now escorting Myra.

'Where did you say your gaff was?'

'In Earls Court.'

'Let's go back there and finish this.' He produced half a bottle of Haig.

'Who bought that?'

'Myra.'

So we walked down to Leicester Square, and took the tube to Earls Court. I felt incredibly happy and reckless. When I thought about my bird-faced landlady, she

41

was surrounded by a mystical haze of irreverence and alcohol. But as Earls Court drew nearer, it began to strike me that there might be some virtue in circumspection. So I evolved a plan of campaign. When we got to the house, I crept up to the front door and opened it with my key, then gave the key to James, who waited in the road. I went upstairs and made sure there was no one around, then signalled James by turning the light in my room on and off twice. (My window was visible from the street, although it was round the side of the house.) A few moments later James and Myra tiptoed into my room.

I apologised for having no food, or even coffee, to offer them; James brushed aside my apologies by throwing the cap of the whisky bottle into the waste paper basket. I found two glasses and a cup; we settled round the gas-fire and sipped the whisky neat. Unfortunately, I was so sleepy that I could barely keep my eyes open. Myra was telling some long and involved story about a friend who became a prostitute after she had been raped by her father. James then told a story about a girl in Luton who had spent a night with him to escape from her father's attentions. By way of keeping awake, I told them the story about my navvy acquaintance Terry, but even to my ears it sounded pointless. James and Myra, who had by now moved to the bed, protesting that the fire was too hot, listened politely while caressing one another. I felt my presence was unnecessary; but there was nothing I could do about it, short of sleeping in the street. I did the next best thing, and stayed in the lavatory for half-an-hour, until someone tried the door. When I got back into the room they were covered with my eiderdown, but the girl immediately sat up and began picking feathers off her skirt.

It was now about midnight. James asked her where

she lived. She said Rickmansworth, and she had missed her last train half-an-hour before. I asked James whether he could not put her up in his own room for the night. He said awkwardly: 'As a matter of fact, old boy, I haven't got a gaff at the moment. I've been staying with a friend in Archway.' Myra went off downstairs, leaving us to sort out the problem. James said: 'Look, would it inconvenience you if we slept on the floor for a couple of hours? We could sneak out of the house as soon as it's dawn. Besides, there's more chance of your landlady spotting us leaving at this time than in a couple of hours.' This was obviously true; but I could hardly let the girl sleep on the floor. 'That's all right,' James said cheerfully. 'I don't think she's very interested in sleep.' From the look of the girl's face as she left the room, I would have supposed she was interested in nothing else. But I said nothing. Instead I took the eiderdown and a blanket off the bed, and made myself up a makeshift bed on the rug with a cushion for a pillow. 'That's very decent of you, old boy,' James said. 'Think nothing of it,' I said. I was beginning to lapse into his way of speaking.

Myra came back into the room and said she had met a woman downstairs. My stomach somersaulted, but her description of the woman reassured me; it was obviously a girl who lived on the next landing. James now left us to go downstairs. I asked the girl to look the other way, and changed into my pyjamas. While I did so she undressed with no kind of embarrassment, and climbed into bed in her underwear. After a moment, this also landed on the floor with her other clothes. I reached out and turned off the gas fire, then lay down to sleep with my back to bed. I thought it would be impossible to sleep; but in fact I dozed off almost as soon as the light went out. I was awakened twice in the night, when one or the other of them went downstairs;

otherwise they were exceptionally discreet, for I was not disturbed by any sound.

I woke up at the noise of someone trying the door. It had been locked — no doubt by James. I crawled across the floor and pulled back the catch (any other reaction would have seemed pointless). It opened immediately, and my landlady strode into the room in her quilted satin dressing-gown. 'I thought as much. What have you to say for yourself?' I felt at a disadvantage, sitting on the rug clutching the blanket round me. So I said nothing.

'Who gave you permission to invite married couples into your room?'

'They're not married,' I said thickly.

'I shall expect you out of my house during the morning,' she said, and went out.

'What about my rent in advance?' I shouted after her.

'You forfeit that,' she said from the stairs. I got up to close the door (which she had left wide open), and James's head emerged from under the blanket.

'Hell, I'm sorry about that, old boy.'

Myra's head appeared. She said: 'Ooh, I feel horrible.'

I untangled her panties from my left foot and dropped them on the bed. I said, with a bravado I didn't feel: 'I couldn't care less. I can't bear the bitch anyway.'

'Hmm, still, it's a bit hard cheese on you.'

I lit the fire, shivering, and then got dressed. All modesty had disappeared in the emergency. Then I repacked my two bags. 'Come on,' I said. 'Let's go and get some coffee.' I left them to dress while I went downstairs to wash. It was only half-past seven. The door opposite the lavatory opened a fraction, and someone peeped out. It was obvious that my landlady's spy system was efficient. I went back upstairs, brooding on my lost rent. To my surprise, James was wearing

44

Myra's duffle coat, and a beret belonging to me. (It was about three sizes too big for him, and came down over his ears.) He winked gravely at me.

'I have an idea. It's important your landlady doesn't see me at close quarters. You go down first and tell us if she's around.'

'What then?'

'As soon as we're on the floor below, knock on her door and ask her about your rent again. I don't want to risk her looking out of her window and seeing me as I go out.'

I was unwilling to confront the woman again, feeling in no mood to be snubbed. Besides, I have always had a shivery hatred of unpleasantness; it reduces my faith in the human race to a point where I find it hard to live with myself. But James insisted, so I finally agreed. Making sure that I had left behind none of my belongings, I went out of the room carrying my bags. There was no one around downstairs. I beckoned James and Myra past me, then knocked on her door. My heart was thumping violently, so that I hardly trusted myself to speak. The landlady opened the door. I held out my key without speaking. She snatched it from me, saying 'Thank you'.

'About my rent,' I began.

'There's no question about your rent,' she interrupted, and started to close the door.

I remembered James's instructions, and said loudly: 'In that case, I shall have to take steps.' 'I couldn't care less what you do.' The door slammed. I went out of the house, and found James and Myra waiting for me at the end of the street. James was now wearing his own overcoat and had removed my beret. We found a café in the Earls Court Road, and drank coffee. Myra insisted on trying to buy both of us egg and bacon, but I had no stomach for breakfast, and James declared that he had something to do before he ate. Finally, at half-past eight, he went off, leaving me alone with Myra.

'Do you know what he's going to do?'

'Try pretending he's a policeman, I think. I don't think he's got much hope. Your landlady sounded a tough bitch.'

I agreed, and we had more coffee. Half-an-hour passed; we wondered if the landlady had summoned the police and had James arrested for false pretences. The conversation dragged. Myra said she would have to be leaving soon for art school. Then James appeared in the doorway; he crossed to our table, dropped two pound notes in front of me, and said with a bow: 'I shall now take refreshment.'

'Did it work?'

He refused to talk until the breakfast was ordered; he then told us how he had demanded to see the landlady, explaining that he was a policeman. 'She looked a bit scared. People hate visits from the police, you know.' He waved his wallet at her, exposing a membership card of the Caves de France, and then told her that I had called at the police station to ask for advice. James repeated his act for our benefit. Putting on a grave and confidential air, as of the natural defender of the bourgeoisie, he said: 'Of course, ma'am, there's no charge he can bring against you, so our hands are tied. And personally, I sympathise with you. I'm a landlord myself, in a small way. Nothing as grand as this, of course. Still, I'm afraid we've had to advise him that it's illegal, what you're doing, and he *could* be awkward, if he demanded legal aid. The alternative, of course, is to let him use the room until the rent runs out.'

Naturally, the woman had rejected this idea indignantly. At this point her husband had intervened (I didn't even know she had a husband), and tried to hand James the two pounds fifteen. James refused to take it, explaining that I should have to come and collect it personally.

'I wish I'd taken it now,' James said. For just as he had agreed to convey the money to me as a favour, the landlady snatched back fifteen shillings, declaring that any bed and breakfast hotel would charge as much, and besides, there had been three of us in the room. So James took his leave, the landlady showing him to the door. Then, as he looked round on the stairs, he noticed a peculiar expression on her face. 'I only noticed when I got down into the street. I'd still got feathers over the back of this coat. It may have jogged her memory, and reminded her that she saw it on the bed earlier this morning.'

Myra said: 'My God, then she might have phoned the local police station to find out if they'd really sent a plain clothes man round. The police might be out looking for you at this moment — for impersonating a policeman.'

'You may be right there,' James said. 'An orderly retreat is demanded.'

We ate the meal quickly and caught a bus outside the café. But all the way into town James wore a faint grin of almost auto-erotic self-congratulation.

Chapter Two

A N HOUR LATER, I sat in a café in Old Compton Street and drank tea. James was no longer with me; he had gone off to transact some business at the National Gallery, borrowing ten shillings from me. I was watching an old man who sat at a table in the corner, snipping bits of brass wire and making them into earrings by hanging beads on them and twisting them expertly with a pair of pliers. He had a broad, good-natured face and long grey hair that hung down to his shoulders, and he wore what seemed to be a very old and tattered cloak over his shoulders. From his concentration on his task, I presumed he was one of those taciturn men whose eccentricity is a sign of complete indifference to society. This naturally made me want to engage him in conversation. (It was only later that I learned I could not have been more mistaken in my idea of his character.) However, he did not notice me, and my attention was distracted when another man sat down at my table and wished me good morning. I said good morning with some surprise, for he had spoken as if he knew me. I was quite certain I had never seen him before; no one could ever have forgotten his appearance. His face was pale and very broad, with protruding lips and high cheekbones; his nose was powerful and craggy, and when he smiled I saw that his teeth were also strong and large. There was something in the total effect of the face that was wolf-like. He was wearing a threadbare dark suit, with a black shirt and red tie. He had dropped a broad-brimmed black hat on the other chair. The voice was throaty, as if he suffered from sore tonsils. He followed up his greeting by saying: 'It must be six months since I last saw you.'

'You must be mistaken. I don't think we've met before.'

'What, not at Tommy Duff's party on the river?'

'No. I've only been in London a short time.'

'Oh! My apologies.' He chuckled. 'I could have sworn we got drunk together once.'

'I'm afraid not.'

He sipped his coffee. 'So you're new in London?'

'Fairly new,' I said, unwilling to admit that I had only been here a day.

'You're a student of some sort?'

'How can you tell?'

'Like speaks to like. I can recognise my own sort a mile away.'

The implied compliment made me cautious. I was fairly certain that he was going to try to sell me something or ask me for money. But I was already alarmed at the rate at which my money was disappearing, and was determined not to waste any more. I asked him cautiously: 'What do you study?'

'The philosophy of Dionysus.'

'You mean Nietzsche?'

He looked pleased, and I was flattered, in spite of my resolve to terminate the conversation as soon as I could.

'Nietzsche, certainly. You study philosophy?'

'In an amateur way.'

'There is no other way to philosophise. Can you imagine a professional philosopher — that is, a man who makes a living from wondering why he is alive?'

'No,' I said, to avoid argument.

'Quite. Philosophy is either a labour of love or anxiety. In either case, professionalism is excluded.'

'What do you mean when you say you study Dionysus?'

'I mean that I am interested in the forces of darkness. You remember Nietzsche's phrase about the energy that bursts out of the earth? This is the energy of darkness. The witches of the middle ages called it the devil. D.H. Lawrence called it sex.'

'Lawrence was a cunt,' I said

'He was a bad writer, which is more to the point. Have you ever read Lautreamont?'

'No. I've never seen a copy of his book.'

'Really! Would you like to buy one?'

'Do you know where I can get one?'

'Certainly. Here.' From the inside pocket of his overcoat he produced a small, black-bound book. It looked fairly new. I took it from him and glanced through it.

'How much do you want for it?'

'Ten shillings?'

The book was certainly worth that much, even second-hand. I asked him: 'Don't you need the book?'

'I need the money more,' he answered simply.

I produced a ten shilling note from my back pocket, and handed it over. He bowed slightly.

'Thank you. Now perhaps I can offer you a cup of tea?'

'No thanks. I've just had three.'

'In that case, I'll wish you good morning. Unless you happen to be walking my way.'

'Which way?'

'To the British Museum.'

'Yes, I am,' I said, making up my mind on the spur of the moment.

We left the café together and walked up the Charing Cross Road.

'Perhaps I should introduce myself. My name is Robert de Bruyn. I also have a right to a title, but I prefer not to use it; I am an anarchist.'

I introduced myself, and asked him tentatively how

he made a living.

'Ah, there you have a delicate point. I am an amateur of old books.'

'You mean you trade in them?'

'That is my problem. If I could bring myself to trade in them, I might make more money. But when I say I am an amateur, I mean it literally — a lover. I have on my shelves some rare editions worth a hundred pounds each. I bought them with the intention of re-selling them. But I find myself unable to bring myself to sell.'

'Where do you buy them in the first place?'

He gave me an odd look.

'When I know you better, I'll tell you... perhaps. Now this is an interesting place.'

He changed the subject quickly, bringing me to a halt outside a curio shop with a notice on the door: *Sebastian Noyes, Antiquarian Bookseller, Specialist in Books on Religion and the Occult, Second Floor.*

'Let me take you upstairs and introduce you to my friend Major Noyes.'

I allowed myself to be led up the stairs at the side of the shop; the house was dark, and smelt of dust and book-binding glue. There seemed to be no one about on the second floor. De Bruyn called: 'Noyes!' Immediately a tiny woman popped up from behind a row of shelves. Her face was as grey and lifeless as old cardboard; she might have been lying recumbent on the floor, allowing the dust to settle on her. 'He's in the back room,' she said.

'Good. We'll go and see him.' De Bruyn led the way through the bookshelves and knocked on a door covered with green baize, then pushed it open. It was instantly obvious that we had arrived at the source of the glue smell. This room was also small, and was lit by one glaring spotlight that stood by the side of a desk. The man sitting behind the desk jumped to his feet. He

51

must have been six feet six inches tall.

'Ah, it's you, Count! How are you?'

Somehow he produced a histrionic effect; this may have been due to the beard and dark glasses.

De Bruyn introduced us. 'This is Major Sebastian Noyes, who has the best collection of occult books in London.'

I shook the hand of the giant, who waved us both to chairs.

'Smoke? No? Then perhaps I can offer you a drink? Try a little of my mandrake wine?'

Without waiting for our permission he produced a champagne bottle and some glasses, and poured a straw-coloured liquid into the glasses.

'The recipe came from an old friend of mine. You know mandrake roots are supposed to be mythological? They're not. I can tell you of two places where they still grow — both in high mountain regions, one now behind the Iron Curtain.'

'Do they scream when you tear them up?' I asked.

'Yes, they do, although not as loudly as Cornelius Agrippa claims. The noise they make is a faint hissing or wailing sound, and I suspect that it may be due to some kind of release of gas. However, the things have the most extraordinary properties. Try this wine.'

I sipped it and found the taste agreeable. To tell the truth, it was not so unusual. It had a slight blossomy flavour (such as I have since tasted in certain hocks), with a trace of an odour that might have been ether or chloroform. However, I had seen it poured, and now saw my companions drinking theirs, so I emptied my glass. There could be no doubt about its strength; I experienced an immediate euphoria, and Major Noyes and 'the Count' seemed the most delightful men in the world.

Noyes asked me: 'You are a student of the occult?'

'Not exactly. It interests me...'

'Do you know the Kaballah?'

'Not well. I once tried to read the Raziel in French. It was too difficult for me.'

'I'm not surprised. But you must read my own short introduction to the Zohar, and my denunciation of the charlatanism of Macgregor Mathers. I will give you a copy.'

He rummaged in a drawer and pulled out a pamphlet, which he handed to me. It was entitled *A Brief Refutation of The Kaballah Unveiled, together with a true interpretation of the Zohar*. I thanked him for it with embarrassment, but objected that it seemed to be his only copy.

'Nonsense. I have a few more around somewhere.'

(Later, when I got up to leave the room, I noticed a great heap of them stacked in a corner.)

'I can see your friend is a man of penetration,' Noyes said to 'the Count'. 'I've never known you to bring a stupid man to see me yet.'

He leaned over and poured me more wine. I protested that I had to go soon, and that I should prefer to be able to use my legs.

'You can drink that small amount anyway. Tell me before you go what are your particular interests? I might keep a look out for any books you want.'

'He's interested in Nietzsche,' said de Bruyn.

'Indeed. Then I think I can do you a favour. I have an almost complete edition of Nietzsche in English. Let me show you.'

I followed him out of the room and up to the attic. Glancing behind me, I saw 'the Count' helping himself to more mandrake wine. Noyes switched on a light between some dusty bookshelves, and showed me several tattered volumes of Nietzsche in the original English edition.

'There you are. I've been keeping these for years because I haven't met anybody who'd appreciate them. They're all out of print, of course.'

I glanced at them and mumbled my appreciation.

'But as a special favour to you, I'll let you have the set for ... what ... let's say twenty pounds.'

'That's very kind of you. But at the moment I haven't got twenty pounds to spare.'

'Oh. Well, let's see. How about fifteen?'

'Besides, I've nowhere to put them. I haven't even found myself a room in London yet.'

'Ah, I see. Well, look here. I feel like doing you a favour. I'll do something I've never done before. I'll let you take a couple of volumes from the set, and you can have them at a quid each.'

I felt embarrassed by this desire to oblige me, so I was glad enough to pick out two volumes and hand over the money. They were the *Thoughts Out of Season*.

Noyes clapped me on the shoulder: 'Come on in whenever you happen to be by. You don't have to buy anything — just browse around. It's not everybody I extend that invitation to. Too many thieves about. But I think we've a lot in common. Come in again.'

I agreed that I should have to, and went back downstairs.

De Bruyn, looking almost cross-eyed from the drink, was sitting stretched in his chair. He lurched to his feet.

'You ready, old boy? Bought anything? Good.'

I shook hands with Noyes, and made my way down. In the street 'the Count' excused himself and went back upstairs. A moment later he rejoined me and we walked together towards the British Museum, which was only a few yards away. I felt very unsteady on my feet, but de Bruyn was swaying like a reed. Instead of going through the revolving doors, he turned aside and slumped into the nearest wooden seat, startling an old lady who was feeding the pigeons. After a glance at his face, she walked away and sat farther down. I sat beside him.

'Mandrake wine,' he said. 'Shocking stuff for this time of day. What's time, by the way?'

'Midday.'

'Not afternoon yet? How disgraceful. Whew, it's hot!' He pulled a handkerchief out of his top pocket and mopped his forehead. As he did so, a pound note came out and fell on to the seat without his noticing it. I retrieved it and handed it back to him. He seemed to think I was making him a present of it, for he said effusively: 'Now that's really decent of you. I appreciate that,' and pushed it into his top pocket. Almost immediately after, he closed his eyes and began to snore gently. I noticed a uniformed attendant eyeing us rather oddly, so I shook him until he woke up. I said gently: 'I don't think you're supposed to sleep here.'

'No, you're quite right. I'll go and sleep in the reading room. You coming?'

'I'm not a member.'

'Pity. Then I'll see you later. Bye bye, old boy.'

He stood up unsteadily, straightened himself, took a deep breath, and then advanced on the swing doors with a stately but nevertheless unfaltering walk. The attendant stared at him as he passed, but he strode on into the Museum. I could see that, in spite of the wine, he recognised the strategical importance of appearing sober if he hoped to find a quiet corner where he might rest undisturbed. I sat outside for ten minutes more, until the cold penetrated my overcoat, and decided to walk back to the French, the café where I was to see James.

He was already there, waiting for me. He even offered to buy me a cup of tea. I refused, sinking down in the next chair.

'Where have you been?'

'I've had an eventful morning.' I told him about de Bruyn and Major Noyes.

'Let me see the books.'

I showed him the Lautreamont. He said with disgust: 'What, you gave him ten bob for this?'

'Why not?'

'He pinched it from Foyles.' He pointed to a spot inside the jacket where a shred of green paper showed that a Foyles sticker had been torn off. Then he held up the flyleaf to the light. 'It only cost five bob, too. Look.'

I could dimly see the pencil impression where the five shilling sign had been rubbed out.

'We don't know that, do we?' I said, unwilling to think the worst of de Bruyn.

James looked at me pityingly, and then questioned me about the bookshop. I showed him the Nietzsches. He glanced at them and said briefly: 'Worth seven-and-six each — ten bob at the most. I expect the Count got a commission for taking you in there.'

I remembered the pound note that had fluttered out of de Bruyn's pocket, and also that he had pushed my ten shillings into the same pocket. The pound note had been new, like the two I had given Major Noyes. No doubt de Bruyn had handed over the ten shillings, and received a pound in exchange. However, I did not feel like admitting this to James, since I felt he took me for a fool already. Anyway, the effects of the wine lingered, making me feel that the morning hadn't been so badly spent.

'Let's go and have some more wine. Do you know a pub where we can get wine and sandwiches?'

James brightened up.

'There's a place within a hundred yards. I'll show you.'

'You must have lunch with me.'

'Oh no. You've spent enough money for one morning.'

I knew this was true, but I didn't care. I also had a premonition I should spend more. I followed James out of the café.

* * *

The next two hours are vague in my mind. I drank several glasses of red wine, and ate nothing but a toasted cheese sandwich. (James insisted that we could get a cheaper meal elsewhere, but showed no inclination to leave; so we went on drinking.) My tiredness from the night before now caught up on me; I sat slumped in a corner, and watched James as he chattered with acquaintances who came in. A thin, desiccated man on the other side of the table was obviously a literary agent, for he talked about contracts and foreign rights with a bespectacled middle-aged lady. This made me feel melancholy; I was within a stone's throw of half-a-dozen publishers, and yet not one of them would take the slightest interest in my work. (I knew; I had a dozen or so rejection slips at home.) It was like tantalising a starving man with the smell of food. Finally I decided there was no point in this masochistic indulgence, so I crossed shakily to the bar for more wine, then sat elsewhere.

James, who was standing at the bar, obviously felt he was neglecting me, and brought his acquaintance across to my table. But the man proved to be an absolute bore, who only wanted to talk about the stupidity shown by managers who refused to let him act in their plays. James kept nodding in agreement, and I supposed this to be the professional sympathy of a fellow out-of-work actor, until a remark dropped by the bore revealed that he had a private income. After half-an-hour he got up and left, and James borrowed ten shillings off him. James immediately bought us both another glass of wine, and launched into an attack on his departed acquaintance; I was too sleepy to follow most of this. Finally, towards closing time, James declared we should save money by eating fish and chips from a newspaper, and we left the pub and walked down Old Compton Street. Before we had gone five yards a voice shouted: 'Oi, James!'

James said with cordiality: 'Hello, Marty. Want some fish and chips?'

'If you've got any money.'

He was an enormous man with a great bald head, on which only two wiry tufts of black hair sprouted above his ears. His voice intrigued me; it was high, almost squeaky; but it was the accent that was most curious. He gave the impression of an educated man trying to imitate a Cockney, and the education kept breaking through. His powerful shoulders were slumped and rounded, and he carried his head loosely forward in a manner that was self-deprecatory. James introduced us: 'This is Marty Roberts, one of Europe's best chess players.'

I noticed that, in spite of the cold, Marty wore no overcoat or jacket, only a heavy black pullover and a dirty college scarf.

His jeans were thin and very grubby, and stretched tightly over his enormous behind. He slouched along beside us, his hands in his trouser pockets. He asked James: 'What's the strength?'

'I've just borrowed ten bob,' James said. 'You are welcome to your legitimate share.'

We were passing an expensive restaurant, and an enormous Daimler had drawn up at the door. Before the uniformed doorman could advance, Marty had opened the rear door, and stood back respectfully for its occupant to emerge. This was an attractive woman in furs. She nodded graciously at him, with a smile that said, 'Thank you, my man'. Then to my surprise, Marty leaned forward, his hand to his mouth, and said, with a nod towards the car: 'You orter get rid of that quick. The revolution's comin'. You don't want to get caught wiv one of those things.'

The woman, astounded, managed to say: 'How dare you!' (She pronounced it 'dahr'.) Marty winked solemnly, and said in his hoarse whisper: 'Now, now!' and turned and walked off. The commissionaire gaped after us.

James was spluttering with laughter as we followed him. (I was embarrassed; the woman's smile had been so gracious that it seemed a pity to spoil it.) He said: 'You'll get run in one of these days!'

'What for?' Marty asked innocently. (The Cockney had totally disappeared.) 'I liked the look of her. I wouldn't want the revolution to catch her with her pants down.'

'I would,' James said, licking his lips.

We turned a corner into a side street, and arrived outside the fish and chip shop. The place was crowded to the door. James began to swear. Marty said reprovingly: 'You wouldn't want to deprive your comrades of their turn, surely?'

James's reply was unambiguous. Then his face brightened. 'I know. We'll go into Osky's round the corner. It'll cost us a few coppers more but it's worth it.'

We turned into another alleyway, and James led the way through an open door. On one of its panels was a sheet of paper that proclaimed in red crayon: *High Class Fish Restorant. First floor.* This proved to be a depressing-looking room with brown painted walls and half-a-dozen uncovered tables. A few of these were occupied by seedy-looking diners. At one of them sat the old man whom I had seen making earrings earlier in the day. A short, happy-looking man came out of a back room and asked us, with an Italian accent: 'Whatta can I do for you?'

'Three fish and chips, Osky,' James said. 'And three teas.' He nudged me. 'You give him the money, and I'll settle with you later.'

I produced a ten shilling note, which Osky took over to a hatch in the wall. He shouted down: 'Three fish and sheeps and three teas.' The foodlift descended noisily, taking with it my ten shillings. Osky said: 'You might have to wait a while. Our keetchen staff very busy.'

'That's O.K., Osky. I know there's a queue,' James said, winking.

He leaned over, and explained in a low voice: 'Osky started this place without enough capital to hire a cook. So he keeps a boy downstairs in the kitchen, and when he shouts the order down the boy slips out to the fish and chips shop round the corner and brings it back. That's why he needs the money first. He's got an arrangement with the fish shop so the boy goes in the back and jumps the queue.'

Marty said disapprovingly: 'He lacks business sense. He ought at least to keep enough money in the place to buy the fish and chips without having to ask you for the cash in advance.'

The teas came up almost immediately. It was strong and sweet, but seemed to be newly made. I was studying Marty with some interest. He gave an impression of latent power. He noticed my curiosity, and asked me in a friendly way: 'What do you do?'

'I want to write.'

'What are your politics?'

I felt this to be a crucial question, but was unwilling to invent the answer I thought he wanted. I mumbled something about being ignorant of politics. He said approvingly: 'That's all right. Better than having your head full of Communist propaganda.'

'Aren't you a Communist?' I asked with surprise.

'Not a party member. I'm a Babouvian.'

'A what?'

'A follower of Gracchus Babeuf, one of the earliest and greatest of the socialist thinkers.' His eyes lit up with enthusiasm, and he leaned over the table to talk. 'You see, where socialism went wrong was in compromising with the industrial city. Marx and Engels caused the trouble. All the early social thinkers believed in small communities where people could learn to organise themselves into a decent society. Then along came Marx, and said that the big cities were an inevitable part of civilisation, but the workers had to control them. But you can see what happens.'

'What happens?' James said obligingly.

Marty thumped the table with excitement.

'It incubates the very diseases it wants to destroy. Because there's no such thing as workers' control of a city. Once you get ten million people living in the same city, they're no better than ants in a formicary. They don't *feel* in control. After all, what's the aim of Communism? It's to make people feel free.

'And you can't feel free if you're just an ant among ten million other ants. Can you?'

This touched a tender spot in me, and aroused my enthusiasm. I remembered the way I had felt on arriving in London. 'But what's your answer?' I asked.

'Get rid of cities,' Marty said, banging the table. 'Sweep 'em away. Get back to Babeuf's idea of small rural communities. Form a society whose only aim is to encourage genius...'

'Excuse me,' a ponderous voice said. We all looked up at the old man, who was standing at the head of our table, his white hair flowing on to the leather-padded shoulders of his red corduroy jacket.

Marty said without pleasure: 'Hello, Jack.'

'Let me introduce you,' James said. 'This is Ironfoot Jack, the uncrowned king of the Bohemians.'

Jack said: 'Me subjects 'aven't been payin' their taxes lately. That's why I 'aven't got threepence for a cup of tea.'

I hastened to ask him if I could buy him one. He said: 'That's very kind of you', and sat down at the fourth seat. Marty scowled furiously, but cheered up as the three plates of fish and chips arrived. They smelt delicious. I ordered a cup of tea for Jack, and we left him to talk while we ate. He was a strange looking man, a cross between a tramp and a character out of *The Prisoner of Zenda*. A dirty cravat was held by an enormous brass ring. He was a big man, with the shoulders of a wrestler; and his bulk contrasted oddly with his voice, which was that of an old Cockney woman, slow, slightly tremulous, as if he were on the point of bursting into tears. He spoke with a vehemence that sprayed drops of water on the table, so we ate with our plates as far away from him as possible. In spite of the trembly voice (which made him sound sorry for himself) he had a most winning smile, frank and entirely good-natured.

He said slowly: 'You'll pardon my intrusion, but I couldn't 'elp over'earing your conversation. Now I'll tell you what I think is wrong wiv the world today. We 'aven't got it up 'ere.' He tapped his forehead. 'We don't think enough. We don't know enough about karma.' (He pronounced this last word with solemnity, as a Hindu priest says 'Om'.) 'Now I've got a little book 'ere all about it.' He produced a book from his jacket pocket. Sitting beside him, I could see that it was one of Annie Besant's books on theosophy. He opened this, and began showing us various diagrams of spheres of existence, astral levels, and so on.

Marty ate stolidly, refusing to look up; James and I listened politely. In almost every sentence he mentioned the word 'karma', which I had always understood to mean fate. But for Jack it seemed to be a magic symbol of all Hindu philosophy and ancient wisdom. At one point he even nodded slowly, and pronounced: 'Wot we need is karma.' At this James also nodded solemnly, and said that he had once heard the Archbishop of Canterbury say the same thing from the pulpit.

Jack took him perfectly seriously.

'Then 'e stole it from me. I don't 'old with religion. They're all the same, all yer religions, Methodism, C. of E., Buddhism, Mormons, Christians, the lot. When yer really get down to it, they're all after one thing.' He grinned suddenly, and tickled his open palm with the forefinger of the other hand. 'The mazouma!' Jack said, winking at us.

Marty, who had finished bolting his fish and chips, stood up. 'I've got to go'. He nodded at me in a friendly manner. 'We'll have another talk later. Thanks for the meal. I'll do the same for you one day.' He nodded briefly at Jack, and walked out. Jack seemed unconscious of his coolness; he waved his hand cheerily, a king giving his subject permission to go, and turned back to us. 'Now 'e's gone, I'll show you some things that'll interest you.' From his inside pocket he produced an enormous wallet stuffed with all kinds of papers (but no money, as far as I could see). He began to sort through these slowly, while James cast up his eyes, obviously searching his mind for some excuse to leave.

He said without conviction: 'I'm afraid we've got to go, Jack.'

Jack went on rummaging in the wallet, paying no attention. Then he produced a tattered press cutting, and handed it to me. It was headed 'The King of Bohemia', and was a short interview with Jack from a North of England newspaper. Jack was talking about the good old days in Soho. 'You could live like a king. A dozen cracked eggs for threepence, a penny bit of cheese and a penn'orth of bread, and you 'ad a banquet.' The anonymous journalist had evidently been at some pains to catch Jack's accent. 'Rent for the basement was five bob a week and there was plenty of room to put up yer pals on the floor. No derelicts, layabouts or bums, 'cos this was a respectable gaff, designed for the enlightened. A flaming brassiere lit up the altar and the picturesque tapestries wot adorned the walls. There was plenty of cushions over the floor for comfort, and music was pervided by a little geezer wot played the mouth organ.'

I was grinning as I read it. Jack looked pleased. 'That's only one o' many. The only trouble is, he makes me talk funny. Nobody ever 'eard me say "the tapestries wot adorned the walls", 'cos I know better. Still, 'e was alright, that bloke. 'E wasn't tryin' to knock me. Now 'ave a look at these.'

He had sorted out half-a-dozen more clippings. (When I stole a glance at some of the others, I understood his principle of selection; the ones he kept back dealt with unpleasant encounters with the law.) They were mostly of the same nature — gossip column items about Jack's reputation as a Bohemian.

One of them was a photograph of a flattering portrait of Jack painted by a well-known society artist; it made him into a noble lion, with dreamy eyes that stared into the distance, a mixture of William Blake and The Vagabond King.

Jack reminisced while I turned over the disintegrating bits of newspaper: 'There aren't many free spirits left. And operating capital gets scarcier and scarcier.'

This seemed to jog his memory, and he fumbled in his trouser pocket. 'I couldn't interest you in a nice pair o' scissors, could I?' They were a neat little pair of folding nail scissors. I tried them out; even on my bitten nails they had some effect. 'Five bob?' Jack said hopefully. I handed over the five shillings, and slipped them into my pocket. I have always had a weakness for cutting instruments (which may be explained by a family rumour that Jack the Ripper was a distant relative).

Jack immediately ordered himself another cup of tea, and James took advantage of the momentary pause in his flow of words to rise to his feet and signal me to follow suit. 'Sorry we have to leave you, Jack.'

'That's alright,' Jack said, rising courteously. 'It's a pleasure to talk wiv intelligent people. Not like your friend.' (He was referring to Marty.) ''E's one of these geezers that thinks they can change serciety.' Jack shook his head sadly. 'When 'e's as old as me, 'e'll know better. All you can do is to be a free spirit, like me. You work to live instead of living to work.' He winked. 'Of course, it's better still if you can live wivout doin' any work at all.'

'Too true, too true,' James said, his mind obviously elsewhere. 'Well, we'd better go, Harry, or we'll be late for that appointment. See you later, Jack.'

We hurried out of the room, and Osky waved amiably after us. At the bottom of the stairs, James said: 'Come and have a look at the kitchen.' He pushed open a door, and we looked into a big and empty room. A small boy sat in front of the stove reading a horror comic. The top of the stove was covered with plates that stood there to warm. An enormous earthenware teapot simmered beside them. James said, 'Hello, Roddy', and the child looked up and grinned. James peered at a drain in the corner of the room and asked, 'Is it still down there?'

'Nah,' the child said. 'They got it out and scrubbed it. Nip got ninety quid for it.' James offered the child a cigarette, which was accepted eagerly, and we left.

James explained to me that last time he had been in the kitchen a little pickpocket called Nipper had rushed in clutching a mink coat which he had just lifted. The police were close on his heels. So Osky folded the coat and rammed it into the drain. The police turned up and were allowed to search the house. (They had no warrant, but Osky knew better than to make a nuisance of himself.) But no one thought of looking in the drain, and the coat had remained there, rendered invisible by the scum that floated on the water, for the past fortnight. James was pleased to hear that, when scrubbed, it was none the worse for wear — although even to me, totally ignorant of such matters, ninety pounds sounded a small sum for a mink coat.

It was raining. James asked me how I felt, and I admitted to being exhausted and tired of my non-stop tour of Soho. (I was rather hoping that James would leave me to myself again, so that I could find a dark corner in some café, and doze or read peacefully for a few hours.) Besides, there was the problem of finding myself a room. This I found most discouraging.

To my surprise, James was positively against my taking a room. He insisted that he could find me kips for the next week.

'Then what am I supposed to do?' I asked. 'Listen,' James said persuasively, 'we can't talk in the rain. Come into this doorway.'

We took shelter beside two full dustbins, in the doorway of a derelict shop. I was damp and cold, and tired of having nowhere to go. I felt as if I had been homeless for at least a year.

'How much money have you got?' James asked me. I was too tired to be cagey. 'About twelve pounds,' I said, underestimating by five pounds or so.

'Well, here's my proposition. You don't want to work, do you?'

'No,' I said with feeling (this was one matter on which I could still muster some depth of feeling).

'Right. Now, twelve quid might last you a week — or say ten days. Right?'

'Right.'

'Here's what I suggest. For ten days, we both live on your money. I know how to make it spin out. Then for the next fortnight, I support you. How's that? We form a league for mutual support.'

'But you haven't any money.'

'I agree, but I support myself without working. It won't be much more trouble to support you too.'

Although it did not seem a matter of immediate importance, I asked: 'What happens at the end of the fortnight?'

'At the end of the fortnight,' James said, 'you would be able to support yourself in the middle of the Sahara desert. Just watch Uncle James, and learn.'

'All right,' I said, 'I'll risk it' I had nothing to lose. Besides, for some reason, I trusted James. Not because he seemed incapable of deceit, but because I felt sure he was incapable of doing anything so obvious as spending my money and disappearing.

'That's a wise man,' James said. 'You won't regret it. Now, what do you want to do now?'

'Nothing. I'm tired.'

'You want to sleep? All right, I'll find you a room.'

'Where?'

'Within ten minutes of here. Come on.'

We crossed Oxford Street and walked through Rathbone Place to Percy Street. Here, James produced a key from his pocket and opened a front door.

'Are you sure this is all right?'

'Perfectly. It's a girl who models all day at the Slade. She never gets back till evening.'

We climbed about ten flights of stairs. Like my room in Courtfield Gardens, this one was directly under the roof. The final flight of stairs was very black, and we felt our way up. James fumbled with another key, and we went into a tiny and very untidy room. James immediately turned on the gas fire and lit it.

'Supposing she comes in?' I asked.

'She won't — not until seven, anyway. If she does, say you're a friend of mine. She won't mind. I've often put her up.'

'Where are you going to?'

'The National Gallery. I'll rejoin you in a couple of hours. Get some sleep. If the gas goes, put sixpence in.' He indicated the meter, on which stood a cup of cold tea with lipstick marks at the brim. 'See you later.'

He went out, and I sat on the unmade bed. (The armchair was piled high with dirty washing.) The room felt like an oven after a few minutes, and I turned down the fire. Then I noticed a razor on the window-sill, and decided to shave. (My own was with my luggage in the Tottenham Court Road underground cloakroom.) So I boiled water on the gas-ring and washed at the sink, dabbing my face gingerly with a grubby towel. The razor proved to be blunt; but my beard was not tough, and it made a tolerable job. I felt better. I started to re-make the bed, but the state of the sheets embarrassed me, so I gave it up and simply pulled it straight.

It was all very well James telling me to sleep, but the strangeness of the room made it impossible. I tried reading Nietzsche, but I was in no mood for it. Finally, I lay down on the bed with a copy of *What Katy Did At School*, and read this until I found myself dozing.

About an hour-and-a-half passed; then I heard voices below, and a footstep on the stairs. I hurriedly jumped to my feet and pulled on my shoes. The room looked so neglected that I felt embarrassed for the girl who lived in it, and wished that I had at least washed up the dirty crockery. But it was James who opened the door.

'Who have you got with you?' I asked, but he signalled me to silence and carefully closed the door.

He said in a low voice: 'Listen, I've got a little girl downstairs. Do you think you could leave us to ourselves for a bit?'

'Of course!' I said, pulling on my jacket.

'I'll bring her up. I've told her you might be asleep and I didn't want to disturb you. Say you've got to go out for an hour, and tell us to make ourselves at home. O.K.?'

'O.K.'

James opened the door and called: 'Come on up, sweetie. He's awake.' A young girl came into the room. James introduced me: 'Harry, this is Jennifer.' The girl looked about seventeen, and was dressed rather neatly in the kind of clothes that people in the suburbs wear on Sunday.

When she spoke, I was charmed to hear an accent like that of my home town. (It now seemed distant enough to evoke nostalgia.) I asked her: 'Are you from the Midlands?'

'Nottingham. I've only cum down fer a couple o' days. I've got to catch a train back in two hours.'

I caught a glance from James, and said: 'Oh, what a pity. I've got to go out for the next hour. But look, stay and make yourselves a cup of tea, and I'll try to get back before you have to leave.'

'Are you sure that's all right?' she asked doubtfully.

'Certainly. Make yourselves comfortable. I'm sorry I have to rush off.'

'Is this your room?' she asked. I was about to say it was when I noticed her looking at the soiled pink underwear on the chair. 'I share it with a lady friend,' I said.

She seemed disposed to ask me more questions about my work. I gathered that James had told her I was one of the most promising young writers in London. But James was obviously impatient to be alone, so I pulled on my overcoat and left. I felt a certain envy for him. She was quite charming. At the bottom of the first flight of stairs, I remembered the girl we had promised to meet in a pub. I called: 'By the way, James?' His head appeared round the doer. 'Don't forget we have an appointment in an hour's time. In the pub. The New Zealander we met last night.'

'Oh, God, yes,' James said. 'I'd forgotten about it. I'll try to get there, but if I'm not, you go alone. O.K.?'

'O.K.' I went down into the street feeling strangely light-hearted; I hoped that James would find himself occupied for many hours to come.

Chapter Three

A s I WALKED down Tottenham Court Road in the direction of Oxford Street, I was suddenly over-whelmed by a kind of brainstorm of insight. These experiences have happened to me at regular periods throughout my life; they are a sudden act of adjustment, a revolt against the world I have been per-suaded by its immediacy to accept. One of the first of these 'brainstorms' that I can remember with clarity occurred when I was sixteen, and had just left school. I was working in a job I hated; I felt bored and futile. One day, in the tea break, I opened Shaw's *Perfect Wagnerite* and read the following sentences: 'All this part of the story is frightfully real, frightfully present, frightfully modern; and its effects on our social life are so ghastly and ruinous that we no longer know enough of happi-ness to be discomposed by it. It is only the poet, with his vision of what life might be, to whom these things are unendurable. If we were a race of poets, we would make an end of them before the end of this miserable century.' I sat like St. Paul, dazzled and half-blinded. I could almost feel a grinding of wheels inside me as some strange adjustment took place. Then I looked at the factory through new eyes. I hated it more than ever, but I no longer felt futile; on the contrary, a passionate con-tempt became my mainspring for the remaining weeks I spent in the place. I was not sure precisely what I was being called upon to do; after all, it was hardly enough to declare that I belonged to a race of poets. But I devoted some time to trying to clarify my vision of 'life as it might be', and the attempt brought me a new sense of purpose and a concentration.

As I stood in Tottenham Court Road, the 'brainstorm' was not nearly so violent and dazzling. I was irritated by the traffic that made it almost impossible to cross the road. No doubt a certain envy of James also played its part in the dissatisfaction. I finally stopped by the lighted window of a bookshop, and stood looking at expensive volumes on art. The centre of the window was occupied by a display designed to sell some new set of art books. An automatic device turned over pages set in a metal frame, and each page contained an illustration. As I stood there, a reproduction of two Egyptian statues appeared; they were, I think, Mycerinus and his queen. Something about their mathematical perfection excited me, and I stood staring. The page turned again. This time it was a photograph of a black basalt statue of a seated man; its form was so abstract that it was almost cubical in shape. The knees and the pedestal were covered with hieroglyphics. Again the excitement made me tremble; I stared at it as if I could eat it. Then the page turned once more. I walked away, possessed by a vision of mathematical perfection that was nevertheless wrought from living material. I understood now what it was I detested about London. The life people lived in this city was designed to interpose between man and that image of perfection.

I recalled some of the desires and nostalgias of the past twenty-four hours: James with Doreen, James with Myra, James with Jennifer, the bespectacled lady in the pub talking to her agent, the pointless regret after leaving the house in Courtfield Gardens: now all these things were thrown into perspective, and I felt ashamed of them. Even the excitement I felt about seeing the New Zealand girl seemed shameful. This city was a massive concrete denial of reality. If we were a generation of moral giants instead of moral dwarfs... what would we do? Tear it down? I thought about Marty and his talk of destroying the cities, and the idea seemed sensible.

But as I crossed Oxford Street my mind lurched in one final effort, and it was a successful effort, like the violent physical action that, when one has catarrh, suddenly clears the nose and makes it possible to breathe again. All at once, insight into my own condition replaced the helpless and already dying indignation. I understood that the problem is to learn to *get to grips* with the subtlest shades of one's emotional experience. Physical events propel us forward, and it is impossible to turn the attention to the real problems. These problems oppress us in an indefinable way, like a pressure on the lungs that makes it difficult to breathe. But we can never focus the attention on them long enough to work out a plan of campaign. The attempt to focus the attention is like the sensation of having some strange object on the edge of your field of vision. You turn your head sharply to try to catch it, but it is still there, slightly beyond your range, still hovering on your extreme left or right, declining to be looked at. Experience is ungraspable in the same way. One can pick up a cat by the scruff of its neck in such a way that it cannot use either its claws or its teeth; no matter how it twists its head, the hand remains beyond reach.

This was also my life. Somehow finally unmanageable, impossible to handle. The obvious difficulties could be overcome: I could find myself somewhere to sleep, a job, food; even, if necessary, a woman. But this somehow missed the real problems, the indefinable emotional oppression, the sense of being in retreat from the world, of expecting to be attacked, the fear of ultimate exhaustion.

There ought to be a way of attacking the world. The enemy General preferred a guerrilla warfare where you never saw the forces against you. So you never roused your will to action. Doubts and misgivings nagged you, but they never deployed their forces where you could see them and calculate the best way to engineer their total defeat.

The Egyptian statues had made me conscious of my weapons. With a clear sense of perfection, of what could be, I ought to be able to define what was wrong with my life. Acceptance was the sure way of drifting towards defeat. My grandfather's death had saved me from acceptance of a 'steady job'. The problem now was to learn how to reject so uncompromisingly that I should never again be in any danger of drifting.

I had just reached this conclusion when I arrived at the pub on the corner of Old Compton Street. I walked into the place feeling elated and sure of myself. It was almost empty. I ordered a pint of bitter and sat in the corner. Almost immediately the door opened and Doreen came in. She looked pleased to see me. I had forgotten she was so pretty. I bought her a sherry, and she sat down.

'I've been waiting outside for you. I thought I saw you come in.'

'Why outside?' I asked, astonished.

'I hate waiting in pubs on my own. But it's nearly as bad outside. I've been accosted three times.'

'I'm sorry. I didn't realise I was late.'

'I don't know whether you are. I couldn't remember what time it was when I saw you last night, so I thought I'd better be early.'

The pleasure I felt about her anxiety to be on time vanished when I realised that she was waiting for James. I explained: 'My friend might be late. He — er — has some sketching to do.'

'Have you seen him since last night?'

I explained briefly what had happened since I last saw her — omitting only to mention the girl Myra. She was indignant when she heard about my landlady.

'Do you mean to say she threw you out just because

you let a friend sleep on your floor? What a dirty trick. What are you going to do about sleeping tonight?'

I side-stepped the question, but she finally got me to tell her about my bargain with James. She had a blunt way of firing off questions that disconcerted me; it was my first encounter with the directness of colonials. Her reaction surprised me even more.

'You don't mean to say you're going to trust him with half your money?'

'Why not? I haven't a great deal left anyway. You don't think he'd let me down?'

'How do you know? You only met him last night.'

Her attitude surprised me; I could have sworn she had been impressed by James.

'I know. But I haven't much to lose, have I? And I don't want to take a job yet.'

'But you'll have to work sooner or later. You don't mean to live by begging.'

'I don't know. Surely there must be ways of living that aren't such a bore as working a forty-eight-hour week?'

I had finished my beer, and she now insisted on buying me another, in spite of my protests.

'I'm going to have another sherry. You can't keep paying for sherries.'

I watched her as she stood at the bar. (An English girl would have given me the money and sent me for the drinks.) The door opened, and my heart sank, for I expected to see James. But it was not James, and I was glad; I was enjoying the conversation too much to want to hand it over to him. Admittedly, the interest she was displaying in my affairs seemed to have no basis of sexual attraction; in fact, her manner contained an element of the bossy elder sister. Still, I was grateful enough for any kind of interest. Then I remembered the racing type who had carried her off last night. When she came back, I asked her about him. She grimaced.

'Oh, him. I had to get rid of him. He practically tried to undress me in the taxi. So I told the man to stop the cab, and I got out and walked. He tried to follow me, but the driver demanded his fare and I managed to get out of sight before he got away.'

'Doesn't he know your address?'

'No, only my phone number. I shan't speak to him.'

I raised my glass to my lips to hide a smirk, saying: 'Cheers'.

She grinned at me, then asked suddenly: 'Now, what about this James business?'

'What do you suggest?'

'Why don't we leave here now? He won't know where to find you. You don't have to see him again.'

'But he's finding me somewhere to stay tonight,' I said, seizing on the first excuse I could think of.

'There are plenty of cheap hotels. Or I could put you up on a settee for the night, if you don't mind doing without pillows.' I was deeply tempted. A single day of wandering around Soho had exhausted me; the thought of a month of the same kind of life was inexpressibly disheartening. The idea of leaving this place with Doreen — whom I had thought of as James's potential property — and spending the night in her flat made an immense appeal. As an ally, she was undoubtedly more attractive than James. And yet I liked James far too much simply to walk out on him. So I shook my head.

'I'm sorry. I couldn't do that. James hasn't given me any reason to distrust him, so I couldn't just let him down.'

'All right. It's your funeral. But you'll have to take a job as soon as your money's spent.'

'I suppose so. But I don't want to work in some city office for five pounds a week. I'm sick of that kind of work.'

'What other kind can you do?'

I began to tell her about the navvying job, and about my previous office jobs. She seemed so interested that I began to talk about one of my favourite ideas — a community of artists and writers who would use their wits to support each other and avoid the necessity of being employed by other people. I became excited as I outlined my scheme. If only enough kindred spirits could be found they could buy an old house cheap, and turn it into a kind of monastery for artists. Some of them would make furniture, others would grow vegetables or keep chickens. The work would be divided equally and they could all devote hours a day to writing books or painting pictures. Anyone who had a book accepted or sold a picture would agree to give part of the money to the community. All that was needed, I repeated, was that a few kindred spirits should recognise their own interests and learn to create a communism of their own. At this point I noticed her smiling.

'Where will you find your choice spirits?'

'Oh, all over the place. There must be dozens in Soho at this moment.'

It was obvious that she wanted to be convinced. I had an idea.

'Do you know the café next door?'

'No.'

'Well, come on in there. We might meet one or two.'

I also wanted to delay the moment when James would walk in and apply his charm to Doreen. So we drank up, and walked round the corner. The first person we saw in the café was Ironfoot Jack, who was seated in the far corner, still wearing his strange round hat and great cloak. He spotted me immediately and waved to attract my attention.

'Who's that?' Doreen asked.

'I'll introduce you,' I said, without enthusiasm. We pushed through the crowd over to Jack's table.

'The very person I wanted to see,' Jack said. 'I need fourpence for ten Woodbines. Can you lend me fourpence?' By way of showing me that it was all above-board, he spread a sixpence and some coppers out on the table-top. I found fourpence and added it to the rest. Then I introduced Jack to Doreen. He rose to his feet and solemnly shook her hand. He said to me, in his quavering voice: 'And a very beautiful young lady. I 'ope she's one of the enlightened.'

'Enlightened?' Doreen asked. I groaned inwardly and looked round for rescue, but it was too late. Jack was already producing his wallet full of press cuttings. 'Enlightenment means to understand the workin' of karma,' he explained. 'Sit down fer a minute and we'll talk about it. Let me just get my Woodbines first.' At that moment I spotted the 'Count' coming in at the door. I said quickly: 'Just a moment, Jack, I've just seen a man I've been looking for. I'll be back in a moment.' I grabbed Doreen's arm and steered her away. She asked: 'What was all that about?'

'He'll talk for hours if we let him. Come and meet another friend of mine.'

De Bruyn was already talking to a man, who sat at the counter, but I saw his face light up with a kind of relief as he saw me. He called: 'Ah, Harry! It's a long time since I saw you. How are you?'

'All right, thanks.' I glanced at his companion. He was a short swarthy man with a beard and moustache, who immediately rose to his feet, his eyes gleaming at the sight of Doreen.

'Let's go and talk somewhere,' the Count said. 'I have several things I want to discuss with you.' He turned to the bearded man. 'Will you excuse us, Raoul?'

'Not before you have introduced me to your charming

friends.' He was eyeing Doreen with what Marie Corelli would have called 'a burning glance'. The Count was obviously uncomfortable, so I quickly introduced Doreen to him. At this point I noticed that the bearded man was holding a rapier in his right hand. The Count performed the introduction to Raoul, although without any of the panache he had shown this morning. He looked uncomfortable, like a man who wants to hurry to the nearest gents. 'This gentleman is Raoul Montauban,' he concluded.

The Frenchman bowed, and managed to drag his rapier from behind his stool and get it into an upright position. (He came close to impaling a bored looking girl who was wedged in beside him.) He then gravely saluted, holding the rapier in the 'present arms' position, and said: 'I am honoured to meet you. My friend omitted to mention that I am the greatest swordsman in France.'

We said we were pleased to meet him, and de Bruyn tried to edge towards the door. However, a new influx of customers foiled him, and the Frenchman went on talking before we could make our excuses.

'I am looking for someone to do me a favour. I have to fight a duel tomorrow afternoon. Could I persuade either of you gentlemen to act as my second?'

'Some other time, Raoul,' the Count said quickly.

'There may be no other time. I may be mortally wounded. In that case, I should prefer to have my friends standing by. Would you oblige me, Count?'

'I'm sorry, but that's impossible.'

'In that case,' Raoul said dolefully, 'perhaps I can persuade you to act as my executor in the event of my death? How about you, sir?'

'I don't know,' I said doubtfully. 'What would it involve?'

'I wish to be buried as near to Soho Square as possible. No flowers, only a modest headstone, inscribed:

"Here lies Raoul de Montauban, the greatest swordsman in Europe. Feared and outcast by a jealous world. Honour above all.'"

I found it impossible to decide how serious he was. In spite of the sweeping gestures, there was something shifty about his face, and it was obvious that the buffoonery was meant to disarm the criticism provoked by his boastful tone. Doreen was obviously unimpressed by him. She pointed to the rapier, asking: 'Do you really know how to use that thing?'

'Yesterday I was invited by Douglas Fairbanks to the Warner Brothers film studios. Fairbanks said to me: "Raoul, you taught me all I know about the use of the rapier. You are the greatest swordsman I have ever met. I should like to have you in my next picture, but you would show me up." So he rejected my services, after feeding me on foie gras and grilled salmon. He understands my nature. Raoul will never speak to the press. Pupils are sacred to me.'

At this moment, de Bruyn grabbed my arm and practically dragged me towards the door. He said: 'Raoul, we admire your courage. I shall be very sorry if you fall in this duel. We must go. See you later.'

'Not tonight,' Raoul said sadly. 'I have a temporary job washing dishes in Lyons'.'

I turned at the door. He was staring wistfully after Doreen.

Outside, de Bruyn said: 'Sorry about that. He's Soho's greatest non-stop talker. He can go on for hours.'

'I found him rather sweet,' Doreen said.

'Madame,' the Count replied, 'you are revealing a curious lack of feminine intuition. No one has ever yet discovered why Raoul is a compulsive boaster, because no one can ever stop him talking for long enough to find out. There is only one way to escape. When he pauses for breath, you begin talking yourself, and back out on a stream of your own words. When I first came to Soho, nobody warned me about Raoul. And after twenty minutes of his non-stop monologue I would find myself thawing into a kind of sympathy. He knows this, and continues relentlessly until you inadvertently nod in agreement. Then you are lost. He steers you into a corner and tells you the story of his duels and sexual conquests.'

We were standing outside the pub as he spoke. I pushed open the door, and immediately saw James sitting opposite.

'Why don't you come inside, Count?' I suggested. 'I'm supposed to meet a friend in here.'

'Who is the friend?'

'An artist named James Street.'

'In that case, I should prefer not to. We've had one or two disagreements. I shall hope to see you later.'

He bowed to us and went off. Doreen said, laughing: 'What a strange lot your friends are! Do they all talk like story books?'

'I'm beginning to wonder,' I said. 'Shall we go and join James?'

'Would you mind very much if I didn't?'

'Not at all. But why?'

'Three's a crowd,' she said, shrugging. 'Anyway, I want to go home and wash my hair.'

'When shall I see you again?'

She scrawled something on a piece of paper. 'Here's my phone number. Give me a ring. Apologise to your friend for me. Say I had a headache.'

She turned and walked off before I could offer to take her home. I felt a mixture of satisfaction and dismay: satisfaction that she was less impressed by James than I had thought, yet uncertain whether she intended to see me again. For a moment I almost convinced myself that she had given me a false phone number, and had no intention of seeing me again. Then I decided that it made no difference anyway; if she felt like that, I wasn't going to be heartbroken. Nevertheless, I carefully copied her phone number into my diary before I went into the pub.

James waved to me. 'Hello, old boy. Where's the girl?'

'She couldn't wait,' I said. 'So I took her to her train.' To avoid further questions I asked him quickly: 'What have you been doing?'

'Charvering Jennifer. She's delicious.'

'Where did you find her?'

'In the National Gallery. She's an office girl from Nottingham and she's getting married next week. So she came down to see the big metropolis and have a last fling before she signs herself away for life. She's going to marry a chief clerk from the municipal offices. So I gave her a little patter about throwing away her life and wasting her freedom and all the rest of it.

And the girl had obviously been thinking along the same lines herself. She got all excited and flushed. Then I found out she was still a virgin, and told her the least she could do was to make sure that this petrified corpse of a chief clerk didn't get her maidenhead.'

'What did she say to that?'

'She seemed grateful for the suggestion, but pointed out that she had a train to catch in three hours. So I told her it wouldn't take as long as that, and hurried her up to Percival Street.'

I tried not to let my envy show on my face. I asked casually: 'Did she enjoy it?'

'I don't suppose so. Neither did I. Virgins are bloody hard work. Still, life's not all fun and games, is it? Let's have another drink.'

I brought back two more beers, and found James in an expansive mood.

'Ah, freedom!' he said. 'That's what these bourgeois

swine don't understand. Take this bloody chief clerk. He's got all the advantages society understands — a good job with a pension at sixty, a nice little house in the suburbs. Apparently everything a woman could want. And yet Jennifer prefers me. Why, would you suppose? Because there's an indefinable smell of freedom about me. Do you know what she said? She said she hoped I'd made her pregnant because she'd rather have my baby than his.'

He looked so self-satisfied that I couldn't help laughing. Then, by way of damping him down, I said: 'But what good's freedom if you don't know where your next meal's coming from?'

'But I *do* know. You're going to buy it.'

His logic was irrefutable. I said: 'Come on. Let's go and find something to eat.'

At about eleven-fifteen we came out of a pub in Whitehall, and I raised the question of where we were to sleep. I was so full of beer that I could have slept on the Thames embankment.

'I am about to introduce you to the Compton Street breakfast tours,' James announced. 'I wasn't sure until an hour ago, but the weather forecast for tomorrow seems good enough.'

'What difference does that make?'

'Ah, you'll see.'

We wandered up St. Martin's Lane and across Shaftesbury Avenue, into some narrow alleyways. James led me into a dark cul-de-sac and struck a match. I was able to see several dustbins and heaps of brown paper. James said:

'Grab a few armfuls of brown paper. It's to make a pillow.' I did as I was told, and we made our way back into the lamplight. Here James dumped his paper under a lamp, and folded it neatly into a small and compact bundle. I did the same. The paper had been loosely and carelessly folded; it was obviously used wrapping paper. Finally, James found two lengths of string and we bound our parcels tightly. 'Now,' James said, 'to Waterloo.'

We threaded down through Covent Garden, and made our way to Waterloo Station. It began to rain, and James said: 'Hell, I hope that weather forecast wasn't wrong.'

'Why, are we sleeping in the open?'

'Certainly not. We're sleeping on the train.' 'Is that allowed?'

'It is if you've got tickets. The train gets in at midnight.'

And so it proved to be. I stood guarding the brown paper while James got the two tickets. Then we wandered off to an end platform where we found a train waiting. We walked the whole length of it — where other passengers were least likely to go — and found our way into a third class compartment. We closed the door and pulled down the blinds. Then James showed me how to tuck sheets of brown paper inside my shirt for warmth. Finally, I tied my scarf round the remaining brown paper, stretched myself out on a seat with the improvised pillow under my head, and fell asleep under my greatcoat.

We woke up in the dawn, as the train rumbled into motion. Then an inspector came into the carriage to see our tickets. He growled: 'Two to Staines', clipped them, and went away. We raised the blinds and rubbed the steam off the windows, but it was too dark outside to see anything. 'Afraid this isn't the right time of the year for the breakfast tour,' James commented. 'You ought to try it in spring. It's splendid. Larks in the sky, snails on the thorn, cows on the wing and all that. It's a pleasure to be a blagger.'

We lit up cigarettes and smoked, while the train stopped at every station in Middlesex at intervals of half-a-mile. Finally we arrived in Staines, and climbed out on to an empty platform. By this time I had removed the brown paper from under my shirt (James was right — it *was* as warm as another overcoat) and stuffed it all under the seat. The sky was getting lighter — it was now about half-past-six.

'What now?' I asked.

'Now we get a cup of char. If it was midsummer we'd set out immediately along the river, but it won't be any fun until it gets light.'

We walked half-a-mile and found a café, where we drank tea and bought more cigarettes. It was light by this time, and we walked back into Staines and down to the path by the river. The Thames looked like steel with the sun on it. The grass was stiff with frost, and our breath rose in clouds as we walked. James produced two hot dogs from his pocket — he had bought them at the café — and we ate them slowly. They tasted like no food I had ever eaten before. James saw that I was half-drunk with the cold air and the hot beef sausage, and asked: 'Well, have I kept my part of the bargain?'

'So far,' I said cautiously.

'Rely upon me,' James said. 'It is not for nothing that Street is known to his fan clubs as the sorcerer.'

'That makes me the sorcerer's apprentice.' The idea made me laugh. I felt so elated that anything would have made me laugh. The walking soon brought a glow to my face. About ten minutes later James said: 'This is Runnymede, where Magna Carta was signed.' I tried to imagine King John and his barons in this wide meadow, and for some reason it was not difficult.

James asked: 'Well, do you think you'll regret coming to live in Soho?'

I could see what he was thinking. He wanted me to admit that this was the only way to live, that I had discovered the meaning of freedom. In a sense it was true, but not in his sense. Still, I was feeling particularly warm towards James, so I told him that London had already been a remarkable experience. At this, he got all enthusiastic.

'You ought to write a novel about us. Call it "The Pariahs" or "The Outcasts". Show how society condemns the men who won't live like hypocrites, yet how they're afraid of us. Look at the way the bourgeois treats prostitutes; he'll go to bed with a woman, yet he wouldn't dream of introducing her to his wife and daughters. Try to show that our society's rotten at the roots.'

'And only the men with courage enough to live outside it can understand the meaning of freedom,' I said, improvising freely on his theme.

'Quite!' James shouted, his face glowing (it was the first time I had seen him drop the bored pose). 'That's the idea. They're all hypocrites and frauds. They spend their lives fighting to make money so that they can buy television sets and washing machines, but the one thing they can't buy is human dignity, because a slave can't have dignity. That's why they can't stand our sort. They know we refuse to sell out to the great illusion. We won't support the sham. We're a perpetual reproach to them.'

He went on to tell me a story about how he and two bearded friends had been thrown out of a Soho pub for no particular reason. The manager had simply walked over to them and ordered them out. When they refused to go, he had sent the barman off for a policeman. I didn't quite understand the story, but I gathered it was supposed to illustrate the basic fear and hostility of the bourgeois towards the 'bohemian'. I thought it probable that the publican had a more concrete reason than that for throwing them out, but didn't like to say so, for James was obviously carried away. He went on to

86

describe how one of his friends had thrown a pint of beer in the barman's face, and then stood in the doorway and made a speech to the crowd: 'You cowards, don't you realise that human rights and freedom are being mocked?'

No one answered, and James finally grabbed his friend by the arm and steered him out, murmuring in his ear: 'Don't you understand — these people see us as long-haired tramps wearing funny clothes? They can't help it if they've been conditioned by television and the popular press.'

James looked and sounded positively heroic as he repeated his speech; it was strange to see him shaken by moral indignation. So I nodded vigorously and said it would make an excellent novel.

'The thing people don't understand,' James said, 'is that all the great reformers have been vagabonds and layabouts, socially unpresentable. Can you imagine Christ or St. Francis in a Cadillac? Of course not. They were like us — wanderers in the fields.'

The effect of this last sentence was slightly spoiled by the fact that we were already in Windsor, and approaching a roadside coffee stall. The walk had given me an appetite, and we spent a few shillings on hamburgers and coffee. James forgot his moral indignation, and told me he would have to take me to the National Gallery and show me a technique for getting free meals out of American tourists. Our meal concluded, we caught a bus to Slough, and then hitch-hiked back to London. A lorry loaded with drainpipes stopped for us, and allowed us to sit on the back. We crouched with our backs to the cab, to avoid the wind, and smoked my last cigarette between us. It began to rain. The rain slanted over our heads, but the pipes froze my behind, and when we finally climbed off at Shepherd's Bush my legs were stiff.

James looked pleased with himself.

'There we are — bed and breakfast for two of us, and it cost less than ten bob.'

I asked, shivering: 'What do we do now?'

'Hmm, let's see, what's the time? Ten o'clock. We could go to the National Gallery. No, I've got a better idea. We'll go and visit some friends of mine in Notting Hill. We might even get some breakfast.'

We jumped on a passing bus, and rode on the platform for two stops. Then James grabbed me by the sleeve and made me jump off as we heard the conductor coming down the stairs. I had not then learned that the correct way to dismount from a moving bus is to jump off backwards, and almost fell under a coal lorry. James steered me on to the pavement, ignoring a cyclist who swore at us as he swerved to miss us. I tried to walk towards a secondhand bookshop, but James shook his head.

'You've got enough bloody books. What's the good of swindling the London Transport of bus fares if you immediately waste the money on books?'

We walked down Ladbroke Road, and five minutes later stopped in front of a large, tree-shaded house on a corner. The district seemed so respectable that I hesitated before going in.

'Are you sure this is the right place?'

'Of course. Come on in.'

At closer quarters the house was less awe-inspiring. The front door was painted a dirty sky blue. Originally it had been surrounded by stained glass panels, but these had now been knocked out and replaced by planks nailed roughly on the inside. James thumped on the door. When we got no reply he gave one of the wooden planks a violent blow, forcing it inwards, then reached through and opened the door. We found ourselves in the hallway of what, at first glance, seemed to be an empty house. The wallpaper had been stripped from the walls, showing grey plaster. The floorboards, like the stairs, were bare. A great many of the banisters seemed to be loose or missing. The hallway was lit by an enormous window with stained glass panes, but half the glass was missing from it, and the rain had driven in, forming a large patch of water on the stairs. The hall was littered with various odds and ends — a tea chest, bits of plaster, old clothes, a broken chair. The only signs of occupancy were a bicycle leaning against one of the walls, and an electric cooker, brown with food stains, which stood in a corner. The spiral of the hot plate on this was red hot, and an enormous black kettle was steaming, half on and half off.

James led the way upstairs. A mattress, with half its inside pouring out, blocked the top of the stairs, and we had to clamber over it. A cat mewed as it saw us, and came to rub its head against my leg. James turned a doorknob, and walked into the room without knocking. It was dark inside. James tripped over something, and a sleepy voice said: 'Who's there?'

'The gas man. I've come to read your meter.' The owner of the voice took him seriously. 'It's in the basement.'

'Don't be silly. I'm not going down there without a police escort. I've been told you keep a live octopus in the bath tub.'

Another voice from in the room shouted: 'Shut that fucking door. There's a draught.'

I closed the door, and James turned on the electric light. The room seemed to be full of beds and sleeping figures. The man James had fallen over was in a sleeping bag just inside the door; he had a black beard and a bald head. As he sat up I could see he was wearing a black woollen sweater. To our left was a large double bed, which appeared to have three people in it. In the middle of the room another two people were sleeping on a double air mattress. Under the window someone else occupied a rickety camp bed. The window was covered by a large khaki blanket which let in the light through various holes and rents. There was an enormous table in the room, and several wooden chairs. There were also a great many empty bottles, glasses and cups.

One of the heads in the double bed looked up at us. It was a pale looking girl with long black hair. She said: 'Oh, blimey, it's the poor man's Laurence Olivier. Go and make us some tea.'

'That's easy enough,' James said. 'The kettle's boiling.'

The man in the sleeping bag said: 'Oh blimey, I forgot that. I put it on about three hours ago. See if it's boiled dry.'

The girl crawled out of bed and stood there wearing nothing but a bra, groping among the blankets and garments that covered the other two sleepers. She finally pulled out a fawn duffle coat and slipped it on. She then crossed to the window, stood on the edge of the table, and gave the blanket a violent jerk. It fell on to the camp bed; grey daylight came into the room. She rubbed her eyes, and stretched.

'Go and make us some tea, James, there's a sweetie. Got a fag?'

'Sorry. We just smoked our last.'

She padded across the room with bare feet, lifted a pair of trousers off the sleepers on the air mattress, and went through the pockets until she found a packet of cigarettes. She then prodded a figure who lay concealed under the blankets on the double bed and said: 'Move over. I'm getting back into bed until James has made the tea.'

She noticed me for the first time; I had been standing behind James. She said: 'Oh, I didn't see your friend.'

90

James introduced me. She didn't seem in the least embarrassed; but as a concession to my strangeness she climbed into bed and covered herself with blankets before she removed the duffle coat and threw it on the floor. Meanwhile some of the other sleepers had roused themselves. The girl who was sleeping on the air mattress seemed vaguely familiar to me; she had close-cropped dark hair, a small pointed face and immense brown eyes. She sat up and stretched. Unlike the girl in the bed, her upper half was covered with a red sweater that seemed several times too big for her. The other two occupants of the double bed turned out to be men, one bearded and very large, the other a middle-aged man with a three days' growth of stubble on his chin. James located a large earthenware teapot without a lid, and took me off downstairs to make the tea.

'Who on earth are they?' I asked him.

'I'll introduce you properly when they all get up. Some of them are art students. The bloke in the bed — the one without a beard — is a freelance journalist. He makes quite a lot of money at it.'

He mentioned a name that I had frequently seen in the newspapers.

'What on earth's *he* doing living in a place like this?'

'He just likes this kind of life. He likes sex and drink and marijuana. He's getting past middle age and he wants a last fling. He's the only one with any money. The others don't mind having him around because he pays the rent.'

'Is that girl with the long black hair his girl-friend?'

'Vera? No. Nobody's anybody's girl-friend in this place. The controlling intelligence is a bloke called Ricky Prelati. He's a painter who lives on the floor above. He's a remarkable bloke. Believes in absolute Communism. The girls sleep with anybody they want to — so do the men.'

'What happens if two men want to sleep with the same girl?'

'She makes the choice herself. Or — if she's like Vera — she just gets into bed with both of them.'

James had emptied half a packet of tea into the teapot, and he now lifted the kettle, using an old piece of rag to grasp the handle. The water that flowed out of the spout looked a dubious brown colour, but I held my peace, realising that it would take another hour to boil a kettle of the same size. (The explanation, I discovered later, was that the kettle was used as a samovar, and tea was allowed to stew in it for hours.) We tramped back upstairs, James carrying the kettle and I the over-full teapot. Every time I lurched, hot tea flowed out of its broken spout and drenched the stairs. Vera was washing out cups in the bathroom. I was sent to help her. She was emptying the dregs from the cups into a bucket — for some reason, each cup seemed to contain about half-a-pound of wet tea-leaves.

'Can't empty 'em down the bath,' she explained, 'otherwise it gets blocked up.' She handed me the slop bucket. 'Empty that down the lavatory, will you?'

The lavatory was next door. I reached up to pull the chain, then discovered that it had no water tank.

'That's O.K.,' Vera said. 'Tea-leaves won't do any harm. Some drunk pulled the chain too hard and the tank fell on his head. He was unconscious for two hours. Now we have to swill it down with a bucket of water.'

We went back into the other room, loaded with dripping cups and glasses. The middle-aged journalist (whom I will call Hoffmann) was splitting wood with a hatchet in the hearth. He was dressed in pink pyjamas. His method of lighting a fire seemed to be simple. He took a two gallon can and poured a liquid over the pile of wood and coal in the grate. He then placed the can on the far side of the room, stood well back from the fireplace, and tossed a match into the grate. There was a tremendous roar; flame lapped out over the floor, burning the bits of fluff on an old square of carpet that lay in front of the fire. Then the flame subsided and the fire roared away merrily.

I asked Hoffmann: 'Do you always light fires with petrol?'

'If there's nothing more explosive available. Here we believe in living dangerously. It's most spectacular, isn't it?'

Vera said, laughing: 'He's pulling your leg. Tommy's discovered that one of the petrol pumps in the garage round the corner can be worked at night. So we get free petrol. I'd rather use paraffin.'

'Blaggers can't be choosers,' James said sententiously. From the centre of the room I could see that it was actually L-shaped. There was an annexe about half the size of the rest of the room; this contained a round table supported on one great ornamental leg, looking strangely out of place in these surroundings, and two more camp beds. These beds were also occupied — one by a ravaged-looking middle-aged woman, the other by a consumptive-looking young man with long blond hair and sunken eyes. The annexe also contained two clothes lines hung with tattered underwear and grubby tea towels. Vera poured tea for everyone, sugared and milked it, and delivered it to the various beds. Everyone was smoking. The man in the camp bed under the window proved to be yet another bearded youth with a pleasant, shy manner and a slight stammer.

Vera opened a large cupboard and took out a loaf of bread and a huge chunk of cheese, as well as the largest bottle of mixed pickles I have ever seen. She seized a carving knife and hewed the bread into a dozen chunks, then dumped it — on a newspaper — on the table.

'I'm not waiting on anybody else, so everybody help yourselves.'

James took this invitation to include himself; as most of the others were still in bed, he had a certain start on them. He grabbed two great slices of bread, sawed off some cheese, and used a knitting needle to spear up several pickled onions, which he brought over in the lid of the pickle jar. 'Help yourself,' he said to me. I was glad enough to accept; all the walking around had generated a prodigious appetite.

Vera said: 'That's the lot of the cheese. Tilly, you and Desmond will have to visit the self-service stores again today.'

The shy youth, his mouth full of cheese, said plaintively: 'Why can't someone else go? They recognise me in that place in the Marylebone High Street.'

'Shave off your beard,' Hoffmann suggested heartlessly.

The girl called Tilly — the one I thought I recognised — said: 'I think I spotted a new self-service store near Shepherd's Bush the other day. Let's try there.'

Desmond said: 'Well, I think you might lend us a couple of quid, Hoffmann. I'm sick of stealing food. I don't mind stealing books, but food's more difficult.'

'But much safer,' Hoffmann said. 'If you're caught stealing books, it's probably three months in jail. If you're caught stealing food, you can always claim that you haven't eaten for three days, and no one's going to be heartless enough to prosecute you.'

'Why don't you just admit you're tight-fisted?' Tilly said belligerently.

'I paid for the marijuana you smoked last night,' Hoffmann said in an aggrieved voice.

Vera said: 'All right, I'll go and stand in Piccadilly.'

Hoffmann looked sulky. Then he fumbled in his back pocket and pulled out two crumpled pound notes. He tossed these on the table. Vera immediately grinned, kissed him on the forehead, and said: 'That's a sweetie.'

The bearded man on the bed was sitting with his back to the wall, plucking the strings of a guitar. The noise was gentle and soothing. I sat there, trying to be self-effacing among these strangers, feeling absurdly happy. I only noticed this when Tilly smiled at me, and I realised I was wearing a silly grin. But it seemed to me that these people were concerned with the problem of freedom, and were doing their best to solve it. It seemed clear to me: the glory and the greatness of human history are hidden from most human beings, and we live like beggars on time's charity. But at least these people were starting a beggar's revolt.

The blond youth came past me, and James introduced me to him. 'This is Robby Dysart, England's greatest poet after Dylan Thomas.'

The consumptive-looking youth nodded briefly at me. He was definitely shy. Then he escaped from the room. A few minutes later I made an excuse and went after him, hoping to have a few more words with him; somehow he succeeded in looking like a combination of every unworldly English poet from Shelley to Francis Thompson. But his voice came booming from the bathroom; he was washing himself in cold water and reciting sonorously: 'Ancient ocean, your harmonious sphere, rejoicing the grave countenance of geometry, reminds me too much of man's little eyes, in paltriness resembling those of a boar and those of the nightbird. Ancient ocean, you are the symbol of identity, always equal to yourself ...' He repeated the lines in a crooning, sing-song voice, in a manner which I have heard W.B. Yeats use on certain recordings. I felt guilty about intruding on his morning service, and sneaked back into the room.

Vera was smoothing out the pound notes on the table, I went over to her, and awkwardly dropped a ten

95

shilling note in front of her. 'Look, I'd like to contribute something to your... housekeeping. You've given me breakfast.' She looked at me in astonishment. 'But a chunk of bread and cheese isn't worth ten bob.'

'I'll come and have another chunk some time,' I said, feeling a fool. James was looking at me with pained eyes. The middle-aged woman, who was now wandering across the room in a dirty blue dressing-gown and carrying a chamber-pot in her hands, said in a fluting voice: 'Oh, I think that's rather a sweet gesture.' She said to James: 'I like your friend. He has a generous nature.' James said gloomily: 'His name is Harry, Harry, this is Belladonna.'

'I can't shake hands,' the lady said, flourishing the chamberpot without any embarrassment. She sailed out of the room.

James said: 'Thank you for the food, Vera. We'd better get back to Soho. I've got to see a man at the National Gallery.' He made a hasty exit. I nodded quickly round the room and followed him. The blond poet passed us on the landing. When James asked him how long he'd been staying in the house, he said, 'I'm not. They just put me up last night. My landlady threw me out yesterday.' James was already halfway out of the house. I thought his exit rather summary, but decided not to mention it. However, as soon as we got into the street, James said: 'I had to get you out of that place before you made any more bloomers. Why on earth did you want to produce that ten bob?'

I tried to explain. 'I wanted to... show them I admire the way they live.'

'Well, it was a stupid thing to do for several reasons. One, we need the money ourselves. Two, when you're in Soho, people like to know where to place you. Now you'll have everybody thinking of you as an eccentric millionaire. You won't be able to walk five yards without someone borrowing money off you.'

'If I haven't got it, they can't have it,' I said.

'You'll never have it!' James said vehemently. Then he suddenly seemed to think better of it, and shrugged.

'Never mind. It can't be helped. But remember what Bernard Shaw said. He didn't mind giving money away, but he refused to have his name published when he subscribed to charity. He said all the other charities would swoop on him like vultures on a graveyard. Now you go and give away ten bob with a magnificent gesture in the middle of a room full of people.'

'I'm sorry,' I said. 'But after all, it's my money.'

'But it's not. Since we're in partnership, it's half mine.'

I had to acknowledge this was true. So I produced five shillings from my pocket and handed it to him. 'There!' I said. 'Now I gave away ten shillings of my own money.'

'No you didn't. If we're going halves, then half-a-crown of this five bob is already mine before you give it to me.'

I groped around and finally found another five shillings, which I handed over.

James pocketed it, with a brief nod of approval.

'Thank you. We'll say no more about it. But I can see I shall have to teach you mathematics as well as every-thing else.'

We jumped on a bus at the top of Kensington Church Street, and James was looking his serene self again.

Chapter Four

THE BUS WAS crowded; James had to take a seat at the front, and I sat further back. This gave me the opportunity to do some thinking. I had to face the fact that, in spite of the exhilaration of Soho, in spite of the search for mythical 'freedom', I was sick of having nowhere to go. I was tired; I had been seeing too much of people. The London crowds still twanged my nerves. There are times when the need for solitude becomes for me a craving that is probably allied to that of the chronic alcoholic and drug addict. It was now upon me with all its morbid force. I bitterly regretted my bargain with James; except for this silly agreement, I might now be in a room of my own, making endless cups of tea and reading quietly. In this state of exacerbated need for solitude, it seemed that the libraries of the world were stretched around me, thousands of miles of bookshelves containing all that man has learned since civilisation began; knowledge like atomic power, capable of transforming man into superman or saint. All this I was missing while I hung around with James meeting futile people and absorbing a futile, gritty experience. (I was forgetting that, as soon as I had my solitude and was within reach of libraries, this vision of intellectual purpose would vanish; I should probably take a bus down to Soho looking for James.)

Nevertheless, I had promised James that I would support him with half my available cash. The only honest way out of the problem was to tell James frankly that I wanted to break our contract, and present him with half the money. It would not now be a very large sum — only six pounds or so. With the remainder I could at least find a cheap room and live for a week.

As soon as my mind was made up, I felt better. At this moment a man got up from the seat beside James, and I joined him. For all I knew, I was passing the best areas to look for rooms, in which case there would be no sense in going back to Soho. So I took a deep breath, and tried to explain.

'Look, James, I'm getting pretty fed up with this business of being homeless. Would you mind very much if I dropped our bargain and took a room?'

'You're *what?*' He looked shocked. 'What a thing to say! You need courage, my friend! Here am I, providing you with experiences that you'll never forget... Teaching you how to fend for yourself in London. You said yourself that you've learned something about freedom in the past few days. And now you want to take a room, just because you turn fainthearted. Don't you think I can keep my part of the bargain?'

'It's not that,' I said awkwardly. 'You see, I've never lived like this before. I need to be alone sometimes. I need to have time to rest and be quiet. All this rushing around exhausts me. You said that you can make my money last us ten days, and then you'll support us for ten days. That's nearly three weeks, and I already feel like a dirty tramp! Look, I don't want to get out of paying you the money I owe you.'

'You don't?'

'No. I just don't want to face the prospect of being without a room of my own for the next three weeks.'

James said: 'Hmmm.' He rubbed his chin (which needed shaving), and stared out of the window. Finally he said: 'I'll tell you what. We'll skip the old idea. I won't take any of your money. Let's make a new agreement. We support each other on alternate days. I support you today, you support me tomorrow, and so on. Then if you want to change your mind, you only need to give me a days' notice — or the cash. In that way, you don't have to trust me until we've spent every penny you've got. How's that?'

This certainly sounded less unbearable. If James found our food for today, then I could withdraw from the contract simply by giving him enough money to buy his meals tomorrow. I asked: 'Supposing I still feel the same by tomorrow night?'

James could see that he had persuaded me — for the time being. He said: 'If you want to change your mind tomorrow night, you owe me nothing. And I shan't mind in the least. In fact, I'll even help you find a room — *if* you still feel the same.'

'All right. I agree.'

I realised, thinking about it, that James had the best of the bargain for today, at all events. I had already paid for breakfast and given him ten shillings. But I couldn't help admiring the sportsman-like way he took my defection. There was something open and likeable about James. He defied classification. Ten minutes after I had made up my mind that he was a phoney, he would startle me with a piece of sincerity or disinterestedness.

We got off the bus at Tottenham Court Road. I felt my bristly chin, and suggested going into the wash-and-brush-up to shave.

'Have you got a razor in your bag?' James said.

'Of course.'

'In that case, there's no point in wasting a bob. Go and get your razor and towel.'

After some objection, the man in the cloakroom let me open up my bag. I took the opportunity to leave a couple of books in it.

'Where now?' I asked James.

'That depends whether you want a wash or a bath.'

'Can we get a bath around here?'

'We can. The Y.M.C.A. is right across the street. On second thoughts, I think we'd better skip the bath till later. If I've got to provide us with lunch, we ought to get started.'

We walked along to the British Museum. The sun had come out again, and students were sitting on the seats outside eating packets of sandwiches and drinking tea from flasks. Pigeons cooed overhead; occasionally, a white liquid blob hit the steps and splattered. James said parenthetically: 'I've often thought that Shelley forgot to mention the chief pleasure of being a skylark. Profuse strains of unpremeditated diarrhoea. The perfect way of expressing disapproval of the bourgeois.'

We went in through the revolving doors. I felt ashamed to be in the British Museum — the spiritual home of Karl Marx, Samuel Butler, Bernard Shaw — with a scrubby chin and a layer of dust all over me. I wanted to stop and admire the Easter Island statues on the stairs, but James grabbed my arm.

'Quick, the geezer on the door's gone off duty. Hurry up.'

We went through the glass doors labelled 'Reading Room. No Admittance without a Ticket', and then turned to the right and down a flight of stairs. The gents cloakroom had an agreeable smell of some lavender disinfectant.

'This is a better place than the one outside. This is only for Reading Room customers. You can have a quiet wash. The other cloakroom's like Paddington station on a bank holiday.'

He hung his coat on a peg, and stripped off his shirt and vest. He then ran a bowl of hot water, and proceeded to wash his arms and chest. I felt timid, and only removed my jacket and pullover. James carolled happily as he washed:

'If I were a skylark
I'd fly through the City,
And make all the stockbrokers
Ever so shitty.

I'd perch on the statue
Outside the exchange
And teach all the buggers
To keep out of range.'

'My spontaneous composition,' he said, beaming at me. Someone in one of the toilets blew a raspberry. 'Swine,' James said. 'They don't appreciate inspired doggerel.'

I finished shaving and handed him the razor. Ten minutes later we both emerged, feeling a great deal better. The uniformed man on the door stared at us; he seemed to guess we hadn't tickets. I mentioned this to James, who said: 'You can soon get one. Go along to the office and tell 'em you're over twenty-one. Say you want to study some obscure poet. They don't like issuing new tickets, so you have to convince them you couldn't find the books you need in a public library.'

He proved to be right. I told the man in the office that I was writing a thesis on Boehme and wanted to study Sparrow's translation. He made me fill in a form, and told me to return the next day for my ticket.

'Why don't you get a ticket?' I asked James.

'No point. I never use the Reading Room, and they don't issue separate tickets for the gents lavatory.'

It was striking twelve as we came out of the Museum. We walked back to Tottenham Court Road, and jumped on a bus to Trafalgar Square. I was already feeling hungry again. As we sat on the lower deck James tossed a coin.

'Heads we go to the Tate, tails the National. It's tails.'

In spite of the cold, a few students were sitting on the steps outside the gallery, eating sandwiches. Inside, a white-haired attendant with a nose like Cyrano winked at James, and said: 'Haven't you got a job yet?'

'I'm waiting for you to die, so I can have yours,' James said, grinning. He looked around at the crowd standing in front of the postcard counter; there were several young girls among them. 'I see the cuties are out in force today.' James jerked his head towards the counter, and I followed him at a distance. With gentle persistence he edged his way through the crowd until he was within reach of the postcards and art books. Then he began to examine them systematically, periodically turning to me to make signs I couldn't understand. But this didn't matter; I knew he was really turning to keep one eye on the crowd.

A plump girl in a white mackintosh was trying to reach over to take a reproduction of a Rubens. James smiled at her and handed her the card. A moment later, he was picking out other cards on her instructions. Finally he selected a card for himself and paid for it, then began to talk to the girl over the head of a scruffy art student; I couldn't hear what they were saying, but she looked amused. I watched her paying for her purchases, and noted the way James's eye flicked over the contents of her wallet. Then they both pushed clear of the crowd, and James winked and beckoned me over. The girl was introduced to me as Leni; she was fresh-complexioned, not pretty, and came from Amsterdam. At the mention of Amsterdam James's face lit up. 'I lived in Amsterdam! Which part do you come from? Heeren Gracht? How extraordinary! I lived near there — the foreign quarter, you know.' The girl volunteered the information that Rembrandt and Spinoza had lived there too, and the three of us walked out into the hall chatting like old friends. James asked her if she intended to walk around the gallery; she said she had already been round and wanted some lunch. 'Splendid,' James said. 'We're just off to lunch. Come and join us.' The girl demurred; she couldn't allow us to pay for her lunch. James overruled her objections. I saw the Cyrano-nosed attendant eyeing us with a cynical smile. James also saw him, and made a V sign with his fingers where the girl could not see it. She excused herself; she wanted to go off and powder her nose. As soon as she disappeared, I asked James what we were supposed to be doing.

'Getting taken out to lunch.'

'How?'

'Quite simple. She's loaded with scratch — that wallet's full of five pound notes.'

'But we've invited her...'

'Patience, my son. I tell her we have to go to the bank to pick up some cash that my father's sending me. I've already told her I've only just got back from Paris. We go to the bank across the street and I make enquiries. No joy. I regretfully mention that I shall have to cancel that lunch date. At that point it's ten to one she offers to take us to lunch instead. It's simple. O.K.?'

'Bit hard on the poor girl.'

'Not at all. For the price of two lunches she gets some of the most sparkling company in London. Besides, I shan't let her take us anywhere expensive... unless she insists, of course.'

'Supposing she wants to talk about Amsterdam. Have you really lived there.'

'No. I once spent a weekend there, which is enough.'

At this point, the girl returned. I followed them gloomily into Trafalgar Square. At the first bank we came to James disappeared inside, leaving me talking to Leni in the doorway. I took the opportunity to explain to her that I shouldn't be able to join them for lunch as I had another engagement. She didn't seem terribly worried. James was now standing in a queue at the far end of the counter. I looked at my watch, pretended to be astounded it was so late, and said I should have to go. 'Tell James I'll meet him in the French in two hours' time.' She repeated the name several times; I shook her hand and dashed off. The girl looked so plump and innocent that the idea of eating her lunch under false pretences ruined my appetite. Besides, James would probably get a better meal if I didn't stay with them. So I went into a pub in Leicester Square, and ate two beef sandwiches with a pint of beer. The food made me feel better. Then I drank another pint of beer, and the pessimism of that morning seemed incomprehensible to me. (This is one of the most ironical aspects of human existence; it makes one realise that all the 'feelings' of philosophers about the universe are equally unreliable.) Being in Soho with James was a great lark. My vitality rose in me; I looked round at the pub with friendly eyes. It would be absurd and cowardly to back out of my agreement at this point; caution is for men without vitality. I remembered how close to defeat I had been a few hours before, and felt grateful to James for altering my mind. He was right; you had to stay outside society, to keep on rebelling. I decided to walk up to the French before the warm glow left me. I crossed the square (where a four-piece street band was playing some excellent traditional jazz — *Tin Roof Blues*) and turned up the Charing Cross Road. At the corner of Shaftesbury Avenue I saw de Bruyn waiting to cross the road. He was talking to a neatly dressed white-haired man. When I nodded to him, he greeted me like a long lost friend.

'Harry, my dear boy! How nice to see you again.' (Was this guilt about his commission from Major Noyes? Or the fact that we had got drunk together?) 'Meet Sir Reginald Propter. Sir Reginald, this is a brilliant young poet friend of mine.'

As I was sure de Bruyn had forgotten my surname, I hastened to supply it (wondering, as I did so, if Sir Reginald was a knight only in the same honorary sense that de Bruyn was a count). The old boy said courteously: 'I wonder if you'd care to join us for a drink?'

I glanced at de Bruyn — feeling I might be an intruder — but he seconded the invitation with enthusiasm. We crossed the road to Greek Street. A few moments later Sir Reginald led us into a small club. The room was dimly lit, but very crowded. Even at two in the afternoon it had a four-o'clock-in-the-morning atmosphere.

While Propter was buying the drinks, I asked the Count: 'Is he really a Sir?'

'Oh yes. Used to be a very good writer, about twenty years ago. He's been in America since before the war. Got a lot of odd religious ideas.'

'Does he write now?'

'He edits a magazine for the Hollywood Vedantist set.'

Propter returned, carrying my pint of beer and de Bruyn's whisky. He drank red wine. I was feeling curiously reckless and happy. So when Propter asked me what I was writing, I explained that I was working on a ten volume work on the nature of freedom. He looked surprised, but flatteringly interested. I glanced at de Bruyn's face; he wore a cynically amused expression, as if congratulating me on the boldness of my invention. This irritated me; after all, how did *he* know I had only just thought of the idea? So I elaborated quickly, explaining that the first volume would deal with the basic problem of whether life is worth living, or whether it would be more sensible to commit suicide. It would range from Greek and Oriental pessimism to the modern German romantics; I should attempt to show that pessimism is the basic reaction of all thinking men to human existence...

By this time, I had noticed the absorbed interest on Propter's face, and began to feel ashamed of myself. I broke off, and he began to talk excitedly. He had misunderstood my last remark; I had only meant to say that pessimism is the immediate and obvious reaction of all sensitive men to existence. I have never believed that there is such a thing as profound pessimism; pessimism is of the surface; it signifies the defeat of lazy or highly emotional men. But Propter seemed to think I was taking up a position of adolescent nihilism. He assured me with great warmth that my reaction was understandable, but was ultimately misguided. It was true — as Schopenhauer declared — that life and time are evil in themselves, and that all human activity leads to more evil. Man wants goodness, of course, but his mistake lies in trying to find it in history. The best a man can do is to be quietly harmless; all the political and religious leaders have plunged the world into bloodshed. Good exists only on the level of animals and the level of eternity; it is useless trying to do good on the human level. Good exists only on the level of reality, which is beyond time.

At this point, the Count asked profoundly: 'Ah, but what is reality?' (I guessed that he intended touching Propter for five pounds.) But the old boy looked pleased, and began to expound: reality is the experience of timeless good. The saints and mystics knew about it. The experience of reality depends on freedom from the human ego and human cravings....

Although there was nothing comic about Propter — in fact, his white hair and piercing eyes made him rather impressive — he spoke with a scholarly enthusiasm that made it impossible for me to take him seriously. I let my attention drift, staring round the bar and trying to look as though I was listening profoundly. In a strange way, I was repelled. Propter was witty on the subject of human sexuality, satirical about the urge to acquire property, scathing about the human need for self-assertion. And I felt most of it to be nonsense. It was all too personal: it was obvious that Propter disliked sex; he disliked business tycoons and self-assertive people. So time was evil and the human world had to be transcended. But looking around the bar, lit by red bulbs, I knew better. It was true that the only thing wrong with the world is human beings. But perhaps one day there would be a new type of human being who would understand that time is the same thing as eternity, that life is a million times more desirable than any man ever realised; that there is no such thing as evil, because the only reality is the power house, the dynamo that drives the world. 'A commonwealth in which work is play and play is life.' On the whole, I preferred Peter Keegan to Sir Reginald Propter, although Keegan also believed that this world is hell.

When the exposition of the perennial philosophy stopped for a moment, I asked if I might buy a drink.

'You can't,' de Bruyn said. 'This is a club; only members can buy drinks. I would offer to buy one myself if I had the money. Unfortunately...'

Almost unconsciously, Propter produced a pound note and handed it over without looking at de Bruyn. The Count stood up. I said: 'Don't get me one. I've had enough. Anyway, I've got to go.'

'Enough what?' Propter asked, smiling disarmingly. 'Enough drink or enough of my ideas?'

'Not at all. I find it all most interesting.'

Propter leaned across the table suddenly.

'What do you do for a living?'

'At the moment, nothing. I shall have to find a job in about a week.'

'Would you like to work for me?'

'Doing what?'

'I edit a magazine. You could do some work for me. Will you come and talk to me? Here's my card.'

He handed me the card, then groped in his jacket

pocket, and held his closed hand over the table towards me, glancing at the counter to make sure the Count was looking the other way.

'And here's an advance on your salary. I daresay you need it.'

I protested politely that I couldn't take money from him. He stuffed it into my top pocket, then sat back demurely as de Bruyn came back across the room, bringing our drinks on a tray. He set a whisky in front of me. It looked like a large one.

'I don't want it. I was drinking beer.'

'Drink it up,' the Count said, winking at me. 'It'll keep out the cold.'

I noticed he didn't bother to offer Propter his change.

'It's not cold in here.'

'It is outside. You said you've got to go.'

I took this to be a hint. So I drank the Scotch in three gulps, and managed to swallow it without my eyes watering. Then I stood up, a little unsteadily.

'Goodbye, Sir Reginald. Goodbye, Count.'

I wandered out, having received a conspiratorial look from Propter.

On the pavement outside the alcohol suddenly hit me, and I felt sick. I leaned back against the wall, wondering if I was going to disgrace myself by being sick in the middle of Dean Street. After a few minutes the nausea passed off, and I decided to walk. Now I felt very drunk indeed, and it was a stupid hour to be drunk. I straightened my shoulders, and tried to walk straight. The idea of seeing James in the French was dismissed; I knew I should be sick if I ventured indoors again. So I wandered on, across Charing Cross Road, and ten minutes later found myself sitting on a bench in the churchyard of St. Giles-in-the-Fields. It had begun to rain. It was also cold. Both these things were a comfort; they took my mind off the desire to be sick.

I realised old Propter was right in at least one thing: the ego was synonymous with nausea. When I could get my thoughts off my stupid intestines and on to something impersonal — like the rain — the sickness went off. But I had had no practice in forgetting myself, and every time my thoughts came back to my stomach I felt sick again. I remembered the money Propter had pushed into my top pocket, and pulled it out. It proved to be two five pound notes folded together. This was the first time I had seen a five pound note — the old-fashioned type, a huge square of thin white paper — and I stared at them blankly. Then I became aware of someone standing over me, and looked up; a tall, unshaven man was looking down at the money. I quickly tightened my grip on it, and stared back defensively.

He asked: 'Where'd you get that?'

I felt too sick to summon, any indignation. I said: 'That's my business.'

'Pinched, I suppose?' he said. He had a most insulting leer.

'Go away,' I said.

'Why should I? I've as much right here as you. How would you like me to call that copper over?'

'I couldn't care less,' I said. I felt I was about to be sick. I also had a despairing feeling that the situation was getting beyond control, and that I should end by handing over the money to the tramp. He must have possessed a sixth sense — or simply noticed that I was drunk. Then suddenly I saw Doreen walking past the railings outside the church. The relief was immense. I shouted 'Doreen!' and started up. I expected the man to make a grab at me, but to my surprise he let me go. Doreen had stopped and was staring round. I went down the steps to her; my forehead was prickling with sweat. In spite of the cold I could feel the heat coming in waves between my shirt and my body.

She said: 'Harry, fancy seeing you here.' Then: 'What on earth's the matter with you?'

'I've been rather a fool. I'm feeling sick. I got drunk.'

I sat down on the wall and covered my face with my hands. It was hard work talking.

'Have you got a room yet?'

I shook my head. 'I want to, but I promised James...!'

'Bother James. You'd better come back to my place to recover. Shall I call a taxi?'

'No. How far is it? I'd rather walk.'

'Only ten minutes away.'

'It's sweet of you,' I mumbled, and walked along beside her.

My feeling of gratitude towards her was immense. We crossed Oxford Street, and walked half-a-mile — to some street off Bloomsbury Street. We went up in a lift, and I remember trying hard not to be sick. We went into her flat. I made immediately for the bathroom and sat on the edge of the bath, staring gloomily into the lavatory pan. She handed me something fizzy.

'Drink that. It'll settle your tummy.'

It did. I gulped it down, making a face, and immediately felt sleepy, but no longer sick. She pushed open a door.

'You'd better go and lie down in there.'

I kicked off my shoes, lay down on the bed, and fell asleep immediately. Several hours later I woke up and found that I was covered with a dressing-gown. The flat was in darkness. Doreen was obviously out. I went out to the lavatory, then lay down on the bed again. Surprisingly enough, I no longer felt drunk, or even hung over. I realised that the pillow smelt scented. I kissed it, and fell asleep again. I was making up for the lost sleep of the night before. Some time later I heard the key turn in the outside door. I expected Doreen to

111

come in, but a voice called: 'Are you there, Miss Taylor?' I made no reply; then the door closed again.

Later still, the light came on and Doreen was standing in the doorway, her coat wet in the lamplight.

'How are you now?'

'I'm feeling fine, thanks. A lot better. What's the time?'

I looked at the clock and saw that it was nearly eleven. I said: 'My God, have I slept for seven hours?'

'Are you hungry?'

'A bit.'

'Could you eat egg and bacon?'

'God, no!' I said. I hadn't recovered to that extent. I rather wished she'd go away and stop staring at me; I felt like an unmade bed myself.

'You'd better come out and have some coffee.'

'I ought to go and look for James.' I guessed I should find James somewhere on the Egham train at Waterloo. Now I remembered I had promised to meet him, and felt stricken with guilt. But my mention of James didn't go down at all well with Doreen.

'You can't go out now. You'd better stay here for the night. James can take care of himself. Which is more than you can.'

She went out. I pulled myself together, and went into the bathroom to wash my face. Doreen looked round the door.

'Would you like a bath? Because the water's hot now. The other tenants use it all in the mornings.'

I admitted that I would.

'Don't be long. I'll make coffee.'

While I was splashing around, enjoying the warmth, there was a ring at the doorbell. I thought it might be the woman who had come in while I was asleep, but after a moment I heard a man's voice. He sounded noisy and happy. I dried myself hurriedly, hoping it

112

was not Doreen's sporting boyfriend; he had looked quite capable of starting a fight. Then I heard the sound of another woman's voice. This was a relief. I combed my hair and went out.

The man and woman were sitting on the settee; I could see from the startled looks they gave me that Doreen had not had time to explain my presence. Doreen introduced me to them; their names were Rod and Tammy. Tammy was a girl who had travelled from New Zealand on the same boat as Doreen; Rod was a big, red-haired Scot who lumbered politely to his feet to shake hands with me, then sat down again quickly, glad to get his weight off his feet. On the table in front of them was a full bottle of whisky; Rod tore off the cap and poured four stiff drinks into tumblers. I immediately refused, explaining that I had only recently recovered from my hangover; Doreen backed me up. But Rod was in one of those jovial, persistent moods in which drunks seem to believe that no one can refuse them anything; he pressed the glass on me. I went into the kitchen on the pretext of getting water, poured most of it down the sink, and filled the glass up with water. Doreen was making sandwiches.

'They're O.K. They're both a little drunk. I didn't tell them about you, because if they think you're my boyfriend they might decide to be tactful and go early.'

While she was speaking the sound of dance music came from the other room. They had discovered the record player. I took the plate of sandwiches back, and found them dancing dreamily, clasped tightly together. The music was hardly appropriate — it was a noisy piece of Benny Goodman. So I went back into the kitchen to help Doreen with the coffee. She explained that Rod was a ship's engineer — they had also met him on the boat. Tammy was talking about marrying him.

113

When we took in the coffee, we managed to persuade them to sit down and eat (by this time they were jiving). Doreen unobtrusively turned the gramophone lower, explaining that she had a bitch of a landlady. This reminded me of the woman who had come in while I was asleep. Doreen said: 'Oh Christ, that'll be her. She lives in the flat above this. She's one of these funny old church-goers who disapprove of practically everything. She has spare keys to all the flats, and she lets herself in now and then to see if her tenants are hoarding alcohol.'

Rod got indignant, and declared that the woman could be prosecuted for illegal entry. Doreen agreed that this was probably true. But flats were scarce, and no one felt inclined to invite a week's notice by protesting. This started Tammy on a reminiscence about a landlady she'd had in Westport; Rod capped it with a story about an even worse landlady in Aberdeen. We all agreed that landladies were a pestiferous species who would be exterminated by any benevolent dictator. Doreen, to my surprise, drank her half-tumbler of whisky neat, but declined a second. I finished my coffee, and then sipped my whisky and water without enthusiasm. Rod found more music — Brubeck this time — and tried to persuade Tammy to dance; but the girl now showed a disposition to sleep. Before he could talk Doreen into jiving, there was a ring at the doorbell. Doreen pulled a face, turned down the gramophone, and went out. We heard voices: then Doreen came back into the room, casting up her eyes. The landlady had protested that the gramophone kept her awake; Doreen had explained that her friends were just leaving. So we turned down the music until it was only a pleasing background noise, and sat around talking. Rod seemed to be one of those men who, gentle and pleasant enough when sober, become boastful and foul-mouthed on whisky. Under the enthusiasm of explaining to us what he would do to interfering land-ladies, he began to describe episodes from his life which, if they were true, were thoroughly discreditable. They all involved doing somebody down or various petty criminal activities; he boasted of being a motor-cycle cop in New York State, and of the bribes he had taken from speeding motorists; he even told us of how he had shot a Chinese boy who had joined a crowd which was spitting at him in some village on the Yangtse. I kept smiling amiably, pretending to approve. Once I caught Doreen's eye, and saw that she obviously felt as I did. Tammy had fallen asleep against his coat sleeve, but periodically she woke up, smiled, and rubbed her face against him with a look of tipsy adoration.

The whisky bottle was empty, and it was two in the morning. I was feeling fine — after all, I had been sleeping — but even Rod was showing signs of wear. Finally he staggered to his feet, and asked me how far it was to the Angel. I produced my London atlas, and Doreen and I spent five minutes trying to discover exactly where we were and how to get to the Angel. When we looked up, Rod had fallen gently asleep beside Tammy. I started to shake him, but Doreen shook her head.

'It's a long walk. He won't catch a bus at this time.'

'Couldn't we ring for a taxi?'

'He may as well stay here. We'll get him to go quietly in the morning. After all, I don't see why I *shouldn't* have friends in my flat if I want to.'

'Where shall *I* sleep if they have the settee?'

'I'm afraid you'll have to make do with two arm-chairs.'

We covered the sleepers with their coats. I finally decided to sleep on the floor — the armchairs were uncomfortable. Doreen brought in a pile of blankets, and I wrapped myself up in the corner, behind the settee. Doreen said goodnight; when I reached up to take her hand, she bent down and kissed me quickly, then went out and turned off the lights. I lay there, listening to the bath-water running, and reflecting on how situations tend to recur. It had only been two nights ago that James and Myra had occupied my bed. I thought about James, and about how much had happened in three days. Then Rod began to snore loudly, and my sequence of thought was interrupted. His snore was like an express train. After five minutes the bathroom door opened, throwing a shaft of light across the carpet, and Doreen stood there in her dressing-gown.

I said: 'Can't we do something about this? Have you got a peg?'

She went to him and shook him. He snorted loudly, then started to snore again. I went over — I was sleeping in my trousers and shirt — and tried shaking his enormous wrist. He grabbed my hand and pressed it to his lips, then went to sleep again. Doreen giggled. I managed to free myself, and pushed Tammy's hand into his. He began to snore.

Doreen said: 'You'd better sleep in my bedroom.'

I needed no urging. I grabbed my blankets, and hurried in before she changed her mind. She came in and closed the door.

'Where?' I asked.

'Are you capable of behaving yourself?'

'Of course,' I said with dignity.

'Then you can sleep under the eiderdown on my bed.'

I climbed into the bed, with the eiderdown and a single blanket over me. Doreen climbed between the sheets and put out the light. I lay at the side of her, with the thickness of two blankets between us, but with my arm around her, and the scent of her hair against my face. It was not the most comfortable way of sleeping, but I felt little desire to sleep. My mind felt like a light that has just been switched on. This was not sexual excitement; my feelings about Doreen were wholly romantic at the moment. Not that I was in love with her, or felt any inclination to marry her. This was a heightening of the vitality by sheer worship of femininity itself, an intensification on the emotional, not the sexual, level. It seemed to me that the past three days had all led to this moment of insight. For this, I had tolerated mere events. I realised that, however romantic it may sound when it is described by unrealistic novelists, the 'Bohemian life' is a bore. The reader of such a novel adds the extra dimension of detachment. But the events themselves, flowing past, have a taste of futility; they are leading to nothing.

Why, then, should lying in bed with Doreen seem any different? It certainly wouldn't have done so if she had been otherwise, if she had been the same type of girl as Myra. Mere sex would have been as futile as getting drunk. But I was now aware of a vibration, the noise of the power house. To be meaningful, life must move inevitably towards climaxes, possessing the quality of music. So lying beside Doreen aroused not merely sexual anticipation on a romantic level; it also made me aware of a rhythm of living that would parallel the vibration of the power house. I had left my family to seek it; but perhaps it had been closer to me when I worked as a navvy.

Doreen was asleep — the whisky had made her sleepy. I lay awake until the sound of traffic and the lightening of the window frame told me it was after six o'clock. Then I fell into a light, happy doze.

I was awakened about two hours later when the door opened. An old woman was looking into the room. I stared at her, startled; the door closed again quietly.

117

Doreen was still asleep. I realised immediately that this must be her landlady. There was no sense in waking Doreen, so I slipped out of bed and opened the door. Rod and Tammy were still asleep — very obviously fully dressed, since their coats had slid off them (although Tammy's dress was around her waist, showing a most attractive expanse of silk stocking and bare thigh). The woman had gone. So I tiptoed back and climbed into bed — this time into the same part of the bed as Doreen. She was lying on her back, her mouth slightly open, one arm flung out of the bed. I fell asleep with my arm round her waist, my lips against her face.

An hour later I woke up, and she was standing beside the bed in her dressing-gown, carrying a tray with coffee.

I grinned at her. 'Are the others awake?'

'They've gone.'

She handed me the tray, and got back into bed without embarrassment.

I said: 'Perhaps I'd better get up?'

'It doesn't much matter,' she said drily. 'I've been thrown out anyway.'

'Oh, God,' I said, 'That's my fault.'

'No. Anyway, I don't care. I was sick of the old cow. Besides, I'm paying nine guineas a week for this place.'

She told me her landlady had rung her up ten minutes before. (The flats had separate phones.) There had been a quarrel over the telephone.

'How much notice have you got?'

'That's the trouble. I got so mad when she said she'd been in here this morning that I told her I'd leave today.'

'Splendid,' I said, looking more cheerful than I felt. 'I can help you look for a new place.'

While we drank the coffee she asked me: 'How did

118

you get into this part of the bed?'

I told her about hearing the landlady open the door.

'You should have wakened me up. I'd have thrown something at the old bitch. I think your English land-ladies are about the bloody limit.'

I was in the bathroom shaving when I remembered the house in Notting Hill. It seemed unlikely that Doreen would approve, but I thought it worth suggest-ing. She was in the kitchen, buttering toast. Her first question was — where did I suggest she should look for a room? So I told her at length about the house I had visited with James, sounding as if I was thoroughly familiar with the place. 'Why not stay there for a few days — until you can find somewhere you like?'

To my surprise, she said immediately: 'O.K. If you think they won't mind.'

I nearly choked myself with self-congratulation as I ate toast and marmalade. At least I had Doreen to myself for another couple of days. I felt happier than I had been since I arrived in London.

Chapter Five

DOREEN TOLD ME she wanted a couple of hours to pack, so I wandered off to look for James. (I can never understand why women make such a ritual of packing; I never take more than five minutes.) I felt curiously self-assured. I was not unaware of the difficulties; I realised that the chances were against there being a spare bed in the Notting Hill place, and even more against Doreen wanting to stay there when she had seen the house. But I no longer shrank from the difficulties; destiny had offered me a token of its goodwill in allowing me to meet Doreen. I remembered Scott Fitzgerald writing: 'Life was something you dominated if you were any good. Life yielded easily to intelligence and effort...' Admittedly, he changed his mind later. But that early perception was right. You merely had to push like mad, and take it for granted that the gods meant well by you.

As I expected, James was already in the French, drinking tea in a corner. The place was crowded with exhausted-looking Soho characters who might have spent the night on park benches. (I was only just beginning to get used to the idea that the Soho bum possesses none of the alertness and enterprise that you might expect; the only characteristics the vagrant life develops are vagueness and inefficiency.) The swordsman Raoul was drinking hot milk; Ironfoot Jack was still making trinkets from bits of wire. I suspected that James might resent my absence since yesterday. But he was as unexpected as always. He met me with an entirely genial smile of welcome.

'Ah, Harry. I'm delighted to see you! I was afraid you'd succumbed to Weltschmerz and gone back to the Midlands.'

With no kind of prompting from me, he bought me a cup of coffee and some kind of sticky gateau. I told him in detail about my encounter with Sir Reginald Propter (taking care to forget the ten pounds), then about the night with Doreen.

'You — hem — find her attractive?' he asked, with surprising delicacy.

'I suppose,' I admitted grudgingly. Somehow, I didn't want to speak about Doreen. I changed the subject. 'Do you think she can find somewhere to stay in that Notting Hill place?'

'Oh, I expect so. She's not broke, is she?'

'Oh no. She'd certainly be able to pay.'

'Good.' He pulled a cigarette packet out of his pocket and discovered it was empty. 'Lend me half-a-crown.'

I handed it over.

'Well, I suppose if you team up with Doreen you won't want to keep to our arrangement?'

'I don't know.' I felt embarrassed. Things were still too indefinite to speak of 'teaming up'. But James seemed to be in an unusually generous mood this morning.

'That's O.K., old boy. I don't want you to feel tied down. You do whatever you like.'

To change the subject, I asked him what he had been doing since I left him yesterday.

'Oh, blagging around the place. The Dutch piece took me for a meal. Then we agreed to meet in the National Gallery this morning.'

'What time?'

'Oh, I shan't go. Don't want to get involved. Not my type.'

I bought James another coffee, agreed to meet him at one o'clock if Doreen's affairs had been arranged by then, and wandered back in the direction of Bloomsbury. On the way, I stopped at the British Museum and collected my Reading Room ticket. I couldn't resist walking into the Reading Room, just to see what the place looked like. To my disgust, the man on the door was talking to someone, and didn't even ask to see my ticket. Once inside, I felt as if I had entered a cathedral. I found myself an unoccupied seat, took down a book off the shelves (it happened to be a *Dictionary of Heresies*), and then sat and stared around me, thinking that probably more men and women of genius had visited this place than any other building in the world. But somehow the sense of history refused to answer the summons; perhaps it was because none of the people sitting at the other desks looked in the least like men of genius. (In the same way, I have always found crowded churches totally unconducive to religious emotions.) So I started reading the *Dictionary of Heresies*, became fascinated by some of the weird sects, and browsed through it for another hour. This left me reflecting that, in view of the history of religion, it is startling that the human race continues to take itself seriously. I replaced the volume and went out into the bright December morning, past the Easter Island statues which stared impassively, as if saying 'No comment'.

Doreen was wearing her coat, ready to go out. Four large suitcases, with leather straps, stood in the hall. She said: 'I thought James had persuaded you not to come back.'

'Oh no. On the contrary. He think's it a good idea — moving to Notting Hill. We're to meet him for lunch at one o'clock.'

She rang for a taxi, and we got the cases down to Tottenham Court Road underground. There was also a record player, which she wanted to leave behind for the time being. I persuaded her that it might be counted as one of her more positive assets at Notting Hill, so we took it with us. She wanted to go by taxi to Notting Hill, but I insisted on paying it off and taking a bus.

Long before we arrived there, I felt an uneasy sensation in the pit of my stomach. No doubt it would have been more sensible to come alone and find out if Doreen could move in. Added to which, Doreen looked absurdly respectable in a well-cut blue costume. We stopped near Notting Hill station and examined a notice board with some advertisements on it, but they were not reassuring. 'Attractive artist's model, available at any hour of the day or night. Unusual poses a speciality.' 'Madame Swishem, expert in physical culture...', etc. I toyed with the idea of leaving Doreen in Lyons while I went to make enquiries, but decided against it, recalling James's confidence that she would be able to stay there. I was not sure, at this point, whether I proposed to stay too.

I rang the doorbell. Nothing happened. So I reached through and opened it from the inside. The hall looked pretty well the same, except for about two dozen milk bottles and a tea chest full of waste paper, much of it smeared with paint, as if it had been used for cleaning brushes. We went up the stairs — I took care not to look at Doreen's face — and I knocked on the door. There was no reply. I pushed it open. The room was empty. The beds were all unmade, and there were a great many clothes lying around. I heard someone moving upstairs, so I went up. There were three doors at the top of the stairs. I knocked on the one to the right. A man's voice yelled: 'Bugger off'. I opened the door a foot and looked in. This was obviously the painter James had mentioned; his name had stuck in my mind because it was the same as that of the unfrocked priest who helped Gilles de Rais's alchemical experiments.

'Mr. Prelati?' I asked.

'That's right. Who are you?'

My first impression of Ricky Prelati was of a huge man with a tangled black beard. He was dressed in a dirty, baggy pair of flannels, held up by a tie, and a paint-stained pyjama jacket. Because the morning was dull, he was painting by the light of two arc lamps.

I said diffidently: 'There doesn't seem to be anyone downstairs. We're looking for somewhere to stay.'

'Who's "we"?'

I opened the door wider, so that he could see Doreen. His manner became more affable.

'Apologies if I made you feel unwelcome. I thought it was one of the bums from downstairs. They're always in and out borrowing tea or fags.'

I introduced myself and Doreen. He left his work to shake hands.

'So you're looking for somewhere to stay? Couldn't you find somewhere more respectable than this?'

'I don't mind,' Doreen said. 'I think the place looks fascinating.'

He went back to his painting. After a few minutes' silence, he asked: 'Forgive an indelicate question, but were you thinking of paying?'

'Of course,' I said.

'Good. That's helpful anyway. Give me another five minutes, and I'll show you round.' He addressed Doreen. 'Put the kettle on, would you, love?'

I helped her fill it in the kitchen next door, and we put it on the stove. The kitchen curtains were burned away for half their length; it was obvious that they had blown out over the hot stove and caught fire. The wall still showed a great stain, as if they had been put out with a pot of coffee. But the remaining half of the curtain still hung there, trailing charred ends in the breeze that came through the window. We went back into the other room and waited in silence, looking at the pictures. I could see at a glance that he was a good painter; every stroke of the brush had a strange, impressionistic individuality. Some of the paintings came close to being abstract, but there was certainly no feeling of abstraction about them; all made an undeniable emotional impact. They were portraits of women, animals, pub interiors.

When he stopped painting, and laid down his palette, I asked him: 'Have you had any exhibitions?'

He merely shrugged briefly. He said: 'Come on down.'

We followed him back to the ground floor. He said over his shoulder: 'I've got a room that was occupied by two drunken painters, but they haven't paid their rent for months, so you can have it.'

'Won't they be annoyed?'

'It doesn't matter. Anyway, they haven't been back for weeks.'

There was a door on the right at the bottom of the stairs. It was secured on the outside by a hefty padlock. Prelati grabbed this with his immense hand, gave one twist, and ripped the lock and its fittings away from the wood. The door had no knob; a length of plastic-covered wire had been threaded through the hole where the knob should have been and tied in a circle, to afford a grip. We went into a small room with bare floorboards, two old armchairs, a huge wooden table, and a large single bed. The table was full of empty wine bottles and a whisky bottle; there were several half-burnt candles lying around. The room was grubby and dusty. One of the window-panes was broken, but was patched with linoleum. A strong draught came up through the floorboards. The grate contained about a thousand used matches.

'You can have this for thirty bob a week.'

'All right,' I said, reflecting that if Doreen didn't want it I would have it myself. I was certain of one thing:

that this place was infinitely preferable to the Earls Court room. I produced my wallet and handed him two weeks' rent in advance. Only one question troubled me.

'Supposing the painters turn up?'

'Leave them to me.'

He went back upstairs, and came down a moment later with a printed notice that said, 'This seat is occupied'. He tore it in half, leaving only the word 'occupied', which he fixed to the door with two drawing-pins.

'I always keep a few of these,' he explained. 'I once had a girl-friend who worked for British European Airways. She pinched me a great pile of 'em.'

'See you later,' he added, and went back upstairs.

I hastened to explain to Doreen: 'If you don't like the room, I can have it for myself. That's why I took it.'

'That's all right. But whose room is it?'

'Yours, of course.'

'What about you?'

'I can sleep upstairs. Anyway, you'll probably get fed up with it. If you do, I'll take it over.'

'I owe you three pounds, then.' She handed them over. At least this left her under no obligation to me. Then she looked round the room. 'The place certainly needs tidying up.'

I remembered seeing a broom in the room above. We set out to clean the room and wash everything with a bowl of soapy water. Prelati gave Doreen a yell ten minutes after he had gone back upstairs, and asked her to make tea. While she did this, I went around the local shops and bought some hardware — a kettle and two saucepans and a frying pan, and a padlock. I also bought a clasp of rather cunning design, that could not be unscrewed from the door once the padlock was locked. Doreen had brought down two immense mugs of tea (holding a pint each). We placed them on the shelf, out of reach of the clouds of dust we raised with the broom.

Doreen said: 'I like that painter. He has a good face. Oh, and he's told me to call him Ricky.'

I replied that I thought his paintings showed a remarkable talent, if not genius.

'I know. I said the same thing to him, but he didn't seem to want to talk about it.'

While I was screwing the clasp on the door the poet, Robby Dysart, came in with Vera. They didn't look at all surprised to see me. Vera asked: 'You moved in?'

'Yes.'

'Good. I'm fed up with those drunken bastards coming in at two in the morning.'

It seemed that the room had been occupied by two homosexual painters, who came in drunk in the early hours, and then had very noisy quarrels all over the house. (I had been surprised by the number of fragments of broken crockery and bottles I had found in the room; now I understood.)

When the room looked relatively tidy, Doreen sat at the table and made a list of necessities. They included some kind of a cupboard in which to keep food, blankets (the ones on the bed were filthy and full of holes), pillows, crockery, and covering for the floor. This was an immediate necessity, because although we had switched on a two-bar electric fire the draught from the floor kept the room like a refrigerator. I discovered that this was caused by the peculiar structure of the house. The room had literally nothing underneath it; it was supported on several iron pillars, between which one passed to get into the side door of the basement. This sheltered space under the house was used as a coal dump. The ceiling above this coal dump was so badly damaged that the wind whistled up through our floor-boards.

It was now nearly one o'clock. I decided not to bother to go back into town; James would understand. Instead, Doreen and I went out to the local shops and bought bread, cheese, pickles, ham, and eggs, and made a cold meal. Robby knocked on the door while we were eating; he wanted to borrow matches. He looked at the food with such obvious interest that Doreen offered him some. He finally accepted a chunk of new bread with cheese, and sat on the arm of a chair. He seemed very shy, but when we got on to the subject of furnishing the room he was full of practical advice. The best place was the Portobello Road; if we intended to buy very much, it would be advisable to hire a hand-cart from the junk-shop across the road and take it with us. He even produced a shabby tape-measure from among an amazing assortment of articles in his pockets, and helped us to measure up the size of the floor.

Half-an-hour later Doreen and I borrowed a hand-cart from the junk-man (who refused to accept payment), and I pushed it to the Portobello Road. We visited three or four secondhand furniture shops, and managed to buy an eight-foot congoleum square, a food safe, two wooden chairs, a coffee table, and even several pillows and blankets (the latter were army surplus). Finally, Doreen went into Woolworths and bought a plastic tablecloth and some brightly coloured cushions. Then we pushed the handcart back home. We unloaded it in the front garden, and I returned it to the junk-shop (which was empty and unattended).

The next task was the most complicated; we had to move every item of furniture out into the hall while we laid the congoleum. We managed to stand the bed on its end in an alcove, and then unrolled the congoleum and trampled over it until it was flat. Then the table had to be manhandled through the door (Robby helped

128

me to lift it), and the rest of the furniture put back. Doreen spread the tablecloth. The bed was re-made (although there were no sheets yet — Doreen had these in her luggage), and the tattered fragment of hearthrug shaken until it changed colour. The room was certainly transformed, but I was not sure how far it was improved. The congoleum and tablecloth and cushions only emphasised the broken window pane and the bareness of the distempered walls. And a draught still came from somewhere or other. However, Doreen seemed pleased with it. She went out and did half-an-hour's shopping, and then came back and made a cup of tea in her own teapot on her own gas-ring. Then we sat down and surveyed one another with satisfaction, but with the sense of frustration that comes when everything has been neatly arranged and there is nothing else to do.

'We'd better go and get the luggage,' I said.

'All right. And can I have one of the keys for the padlock?'

'You'd better have them both,' I said. 'It's your room.'

'No. You keep one. But... there's only one thing...'

'What's that?'

'Well — if it's my room, I don't want James spending half his time here.'

'That's all right. It's your room.'

'It's not that I dislike James. But... you understand...'

I didn't, but I didn't say so. I didn't want to discuss it at this point, because I knew we were both exhausted. It had been a long day. Every muscle in my body ached. I poured more tea, and lay down on the bed, closing my eyes. Doreen asked: 'Shall we go?'

'Hadn't we better wait? It's the rush hour now.'

She put out the light, and lay beside me. The bars of the fire made a red glare on the ceiling. Cars went up and down the road outside, their headlights illuminating the room. In the hall outside people were talking and clattering around. But the door was fastened on the inside (it had a hook-and-eye catch), and we were both tired. The noise only insulated me in the world in which I lay beside Doreen. At first, I was too excited by her presence beside me to feel like sleeping; but when I put my arm round her she firmly grasped my hand, and fell asleep with it pressed against her. Then I slept too.

It must have been about an hour later when I was wakened by someone knocking on the door. James's voice called: 'Are you in, old boy?' I lay there, rising slowly to the surface. James didn't knock again; I heard his footsteps mounting the stairs. I crossed to the door and opened it, blinking in the light. James said: 'Ah, there you are. Don't let me disturb you.'

I closed the door behind me, so as not to disturb Doreen, and stood there in my stockinged feet, rubbing my eyes. James came down again.

'I saw the light was off, so I didn't want to wake you up. Where's Doreen?'

I jerked my head towards the door. James said: 'Ah, I see.'

I was rather glad he had the wrong idea. It made me feel less guilty about deserting him. Briefly, I explained why we hadn't appeared at lunch time. He asked: 'Will you share the room with her?'

'If she'll let me,' I said.

He nodded approval. I asked him what he intended to do now.

'I'm just leaving anyway. I've been here for half-an-hour. Do you want to come and help me busk a theatre queue?'

'How?'

'I'll show you. We'll make enough money for a few beers.'

'I owe you supper,' I said, remembering my responsibility.

'Pooh, forget it. You have other — ahem — irons in the fire.'

I went in and gently shook Doreen awake. I asked her to give me the cloakroom ticket for her cases; I could bring them back. She murmured sleepily about a handbag. I found the ticket, covered her with a blanket, and kissed her. James and I walked up to Notting Hill station. The prospect of busking a theatre queue did not appeal to me, but I felt I owed it to James to turn up and support him.

We got off at Tottenham Court Road and walked down to the Princes. Although I was apparently supposed to do nothing but collect the money, I already felt a fluttering in the stomach. James seemed unconcerned. He glanced at a clock, and commented: 'Seven o'clock. Time to do another queue after this one.'

But we had been forestalled. In the middle of the road outside the theatre three men were doing a vigorous song and dance act. The sounds of the accordion reached us from a hundred yards away. I felt relieved. We stood and watched them for five minutes. The act was good. Two men in pinstriped suits and bowler hats sang and tap danced in perfect unison; then they abandoned their hats and jackets and pulled on shawls and turbans; the accordion made noises like a bamboo flute, and they began a sinuous and comic Hindu dance. We left when another little man approached us with a hat. James said: 'Never mind. We'll go down St. Martin's Lane.'

We found a bored-looking queue outside the New Theatre. James stood six feet away, and announced in a loud voice: 'Ladies and gentlemen, until you move into the theatre I shall endeavour to entertain you.' No one said anything. I half-expected some sarcastic remarks. James went on, with no sign of nervousness: 'As some of you will remember, ladies and gentlemen, my speciality is the Elizabethan drama. No doubt some of you possess the works of Marlowe that I edited for the Foot and Mouth Press.' The audience laughed; James had obviously gauged them perfectly by the play they were going to see (a rather highbrow piece, translated from the French). 'Unfortunately, while I was studying for my finals at RADA, the school was struck by a V.2 rocket. I paid no attention — I thought it was the result of taking bicarbonate of soda on an empty stomach. But when I woke up in hospital two days later, I realised that I no longer remembered which plays of Shakespeare the various lines came from. I think I have more or less overcome this affliction; but in case I haven't, I trust you will overlook my little slips. Ahem.'

He started to recite an ingenious farrago of Shakespeare and other Elizabethan dramatists, which I can no longer remember in detail. He began with 'The quality of mercy,' and rambled on to 'Once more into the breach, dear friends', but when he got to the line about 'God for England, Harry and St. George', substituted 'Was this the face that launched a thousand ships?', and intermixed this with quotations from 'My Fair Lady'. It was obvious that he touched a strand of cultural snobbery in his audience, for they laughed loudly as he switched from one play to another, even if the change had no particular comic effect. When he came to the end of the speech, they applauded loudly. James announced that, during his next recitation, his colleague would pass among them with the Box Office. I had improvised a hat out of a newspaper, and started at the end of the queue. Meanwhile, James went on to say that he was at present working on a scheme to raise the tone of ITV advertisements, and had persuaded his boss to allow him to try a new method of using Shakespeare on the air. This, for example, was his idea for advertising a famous laxative. He began: 'To squeeze or not to squeeze, that is the question ...' Some of his lines steered pretty close to crudity, without actually being offensive. But the audience was thoroughly sympathetic by this time. In a break for applause, James beckoned me over, and told me to start at the front of the queue, as the audience was about to start moving in. He then went on to recite speeches from what he claimed to be Shaw's greatest play, *The Admirable Bashville*. The queue moved in, and I collected what felt like half-a-hundredweight of coppers. Five minutes later, we were left alone. I told James enthusiastically that he was brilliant, and he looked gratified. When I asked who wrote his material, he explained lightly that it was traditional. We went into the pub opposite, found a corner table, and counted the money while we drank pints of bitter. There was about eight shillings, mostly in pennies and ha'pennies.

'But what do you do if the queue's waiting to see a knockabout farce?' I asked him.

'Give 'em *Eskimo Nell* or *Christmas Day in the Workhouse*. And if it's a queue outside the Old Vic, I make a speech telling them they ought to know more about the other Elizabethan dramatists. Then I give 'em the rabble-rousing bits out of Marlowe's *Tamburlaine* and *The Spanish Tragedy*. You just have to guess the mood of your audience. William McGonagal's usually a big hit with the highbrow audiences.'

James never ceased to surprise me with new aspects of himself. I pointed out that if he did this twice a night, he'd be able to make some sort of a living.

'But who wants to? If I did it every day, I'd cease to enjoy it. I'd become a professional instead of an amateur.

Anyway, I'd begin to feel that the queues had heard my act more than once. That'd spoil the fun. As it is, I have about fifty different ways of making a few bob. It'd take me weeks to show them all to you.'

I realised then that the theatre performance had been put on specially for me. It was James's attempt to persuade me away from Doreen. However, I preferred not to see this. I noticed they sold ham sandwiches at the counter, so I bought a couple, and two more pints of bitter. James's success with the theatre queue positively inspired him. He began to explain at length to me the philosophy of freedom. For the first time, I realised that it was really a kind of vision, and not just an excuse for doing nothing. I asked him when he had first had the idea.

'I can tell you that quite exactly. When I got out of the army, I came to Soho with a couple of quid in my pocket. On my first evening I met a girl in a pub — I went and offered to sketch her. One of these art school types. She obviously wanted to slip between the sheets, and I felt my usual noblesse oblige. The trouble was, she lived in Balham or somewhere with her parents, and I was sleeping on somebody's floor. She could say she was staying in town with friends, but we had nowhere to sleep. Well, we wandered around for an hour, then somebody told us about an empty cinema behind the Tottenham Court Road. Used to be next door to Woolworths. So we went to this place and slept on the floor — there weren't any seats in it, of course. It rained in the night and we had to change our positions because the rain came in. We found a roll of lagging in one of the lavatories — you know, the stuff you wrap round pipes in the winter — and we used it for a mattress. She was all right in bed... on the floor, I should say. Well, early the next morning, I got up — left her to make her own way back to art school — and went out. It was one of those drizzly wet mornings in summer — you know the kind I mean. Well, I found a sackful of hot rolls outside a café, and pinched a couple; then I pinched a bottle of milk off a doorstep further down the street. Then I stood there in a doorway in the rain, and watched the poor sods on their way to work, hurrying through the rain. Well, that's when it first happened.'

'*What* happened?' I persisted. I was struck by his sincerity; he was obviously trying to remember exactly what it was like as he talked.

'There they were, all on their way to make money for the boss. They'd got caught in the big machine. They didn't know what it was like to be alive, to be free. They just never get a chance to find out from the moment they're born. They get educated. That's the trouble. Big Brother tells 'em they've got to serve the community, work for society and all that blag. They've been brainwashed, and they never find out. And what's the good of telling 'em they've all been twisted out of shape? I wouldn't *like* everybody to be like me. What's the good? We need people like that, just as we need sheep to kill for dinner. But I'm not going to join in the game. I'd rather be free.'

'Man is born free, and he's everywhere in chains,' I quoted.

'That's right,' James said. 'You get some very good ideas sometimes. Man is born free and he's everywhere in chains... That's good.'

I could see I was in for another peroration, so I emptied my glass and suggested we should move on. We walked up to Soho, looked into the French, which was crowded, and ducked out again when Raoul spotted us and started to elbow his way towards us. I mentioned the club I had been in the day before, and asked James if he knew it.

135

'The Caves? Yes, I'm a member. Let's go in there for a drink if you like.'

In the doorway we bumped into a short fat man and a tall thin man, both very drunk; they were harmonising 'When you come home again to Wales'. When we had pushed past them James muttered in my ear, 'That's Davis and Jones, the two painters you've evicted from their room.' I was horrified. I looked after them — they had only progressed a few feet. The tall man looked more like a consumptive window-cleaner; he had a narrow, boney face, with a beaky nose and bright eyes. The short man had a strange, stodgy appearance; his square-ish face looked ruddy and healthy; he had a small, square moustache and enormous eyelids that at the moment were almost closed. James sketched in their history for me; they had been discovered in Cardiff five years before by a famous art critic; they had come to London and had one highly successful exhibition, and had been drunk ever since.

'Do you think they'll make trouble?' I asked.

'Only if they remember where they live. Apparently they haven't been back there for several weeks, so probably they've forgotten. If they turn up, tell them they're mistaken. Say you've been living in that room for the past five years.'

James bought two pints, and we looked round for a seat. Then I saw Sir Reginald Propter sitting in a corner, talking to a large woman dressed in a blue cloak. He saw me across the room, and smiled. 'Friend of yours?' James asked, and then his expression changed. As I started to move away from the bar, he grabbed my sleeve. 'Don't go over there. That woman's one of the worst bitches in Soho. She's a Christian soul-saver.'

But Propter was beckoning to me; I shrugged helplessly, and went over. He stood up.

'Hello, Harry.' (I was flattered that he used my name as if we were old friends.) 'I'd like you to meet Barbara Collifax. She's a fine poetess.'

The woman reached a gloved hand over to me. At close quarters she was strikingly ugly, with a raw-boned face and gravestone teeth. She said, in a voice that was almost a bass: 'I think we know each other, don't we?'

'I don't think so.'

'Didn't you once ask me a question about the after-life at the end of a lecture?'

I assured her I never had. She looked as if she didn't believe me. She said: 'Well, I presume, since my friend Reggie wanted me to meet you, we must have some common interest.'

'You have,' Propter said. 'Harry is writing a book on the spiritual predicament of modern man.'

'Really. Do sit down and tell me about it.'

I looked back at James. 'I'm afraid I ought to go back to my friend.'

She peered short-sightedly across the room and said: 'Won't he come over too?'

'I'll ask him.' I tried beckoning to James across the room. Reluctantly, he came over. The woman stared at him blankly, and then said: 'Oh, it's you.'

'It's nice to see you again too,' James said.

She blinked as if he had slapped her face, then glared at him with fury.

'I don't think I like your impertinence!'

'Then I'll remove it to a place where you won't inspire it,' James said, smiling blandly.

Sir Reginald, looking embarrassed and alarmed, said quickly: 'Come, come. I don't think any offence was intended.'

I introduced James to Propter. Looking thoroughly unhappy, he said: 'Won't you sit down?'

The woman rose majestically to her feet. She said, in her resounding voice: 'I shall leave.'

I thought for a moment she'd let it go at that; but she glared at James, and then declared: 'The company of flippant imbeciles is worse than no company at all.'

She ignored Propter's attempt to detain her, and walked out. I saw an expression of unmistakable relief on Propter's face as he looked after her. I sat down. Propter looked at James with mild surprise.

'Whatever have you done to her?'

'Nothing. She tried to convert me once, and I expounded my — er — philosophy of freedom.'

'She's terribly serious-minded,' Propter agreed. The words had an air of understatement.

'I'm sorry if I've spoilt your evening,' James said. He was fishing for more information about the woman.

'You haven't. I was trying to persuade her to write an article for me. She's an expert on the cult of Mithras. Unfortunately, she seems to hold strong ideas on the wickedness of Buddhism. So we were both beginning to feel uncomfortable.'

'She'll probably come back in five minutes to apologise,' James said.

'Do you think so?'

'I think so. I know her fairly well.'

'Then I think we'd better leave.'

We both emptied our glasses and followed Propter out. I realised now why he had beckoned me over with such friendliness. He looked up and down Dean Street, then hailed a passing taxi. I said: 'Perhaps we'd better leave you?'

'Not unless you're busy. Let's go and have a drink somewhere else.'

We piled into the taxi. Propter told the driver to go to Fitzroy Square. James asked him where he was living.

'In Clanricarde Gardens.'

'Really? That's near Harry's new place. Why don't you come back and have a drink with us?'

I glanced at James, wondering what he had in mind. It was a logical assumption that the invitation was not entirely disinterested. And although I felt reasonably proud of Doreen's room, I didn't feel like inviting a baronet to drink beer in it. Propter accepted the invitation at its face value.

'That's very kind of you. I think I won't stay long, though. I'm rather tired.'

As we waited at the Oxford Street traffic lights, I remembered Doreen's bags, and asked Propter if he would mind waiting while we collected them. James and I descended into the Tottenham Court Road underground.

'What's the idea?' I asked him.

'No idea. He seems a decent bloke. May as well get to know him better. Besides, I bet he's interested in painting. We might do Ricky Prelati a good turn.'

I was getting too accustomed to the intricacies of James's character to be surprised by these altruistic sentiments. Then he added: 'Anyway, he's bound to provide some of the booze.'

We got the cases — and my own luggage — up to the taxi. Half-way to Notting Hill, James asked: 'By the way, Harry, is there any drink on your premises?'

'Not yet. I only moved in today. We'll stop and get some.'

James's reading of Propter's character had been correct. When the taxi stopped opposite the house, we went into the pub next door. I bought two quarts of ale and some Spanish burgundy. Propter insisted on buying a bottle of whisky.

James asked Propter: 'Are you interested in painting?'

'Very much so.'

'Then you ought to see the work of a bloke who lives here. He's talented.'

I saw a look of caution flit across Propter's face; no doubt he had been lured into this kind of thing before — situations in which the only defence is to say you've forgotten your cheque book. Between us, we got the bags and bottles into the hall. The door of Doreen's room was locked. I opened it with my key; the light and fire had been left on.

'This is comfortable,' Propter said. He was looking around the room with a benevolent and reminiscent stare. James went off upstairs to see who was in. A moment later he called, 'Come on up. They're all here.' We took the bottles upstairs.

The room looked different in the evening. The naked electric bulbs gave it a bright glare. The curtains had been taken down from the windows; only a leafless tree outside obstructed the view of the people who lived in the block of luxury flats over the road. There was a good fire burning in the grate, and a strong smell of cooking and garlic. Most of the people in the room were the ones I had seen before, although there were a few new faces among them. Hoffmann, the journalist, lay on the bed, looking very ill and tired. Doreen was sitting on a chair near the fire (I recognised it as one from her own room), drinking a glass of white wine. The beds and chairs had been arranged to leave a large circle in the middle of the room; this was occupied by an array of bottles — beer bottles and cheap burgundy and sauterne.

Our appearance — loaded with bottles — was greeted with cheerful shouts. Doreen caught my eye and smiled. I was glad she had chosen a chair on her own in the corner; the other women in the room were distributed on various beds among the men, who out-numbered them. James introduced Propter to the company by simply announcing his name loudly.

'I can't be bothered to tell you everybody's name. Address the men as daddy-o and the women as toots.'

Someone vacated a chair for Propter and offered him a cup without a handle. Desmond — the youth who had been delegated to steal food the previous day — seemed to have lost his shyness with the wine. He called to me: 'Did you bring Doreen's record player?' When I nodded, he said: 'Hooray, let's have music.'

Doreen threaded her way across the room, and we went downstairs. I asked her: 'How do you like them?'

'They're funny. I've never seen anything like that in New Zealand. I'm glad I came here.'

She opened up one of her cases and took out records. At this point I turned her round and kissed her. She pushed me away, saying: 'Don't. We can be seen.'

I reached over and switched out the light, then kissed her again. She relaxed against me, and her lips parted. I found it hard to let her go, and went on kissing her until we both felt slightly feverish. She disengaged herself.

'Come on. We don't want to get like that lot upstairs.'

She switched the light on, and I picked up the records, trying not to look as disturbed as I felt. I asked, trying to sound casual: 'Why, what's wrong with them?'

'Oh, nothing. But they're pretty open about it, aren't they? That girl Vera started drinking wine and kissing Tommy with her mouth full of it. After a few minutes of that, they just got up and went out of the room. I think if she'd been a bit more drunk they wouldn't have bothered to leave the room.'

I could see that living in this place might have its disadvantages if it brought out the prude in Doreen. But it was too early to say. We took the record player back upstairs. Desmond plunged on the records with a yell of delight; within a few minutes all conversation was drowned by the Brubeck octet, turned up as loud as it would go.

Robby Dysart, it appeared, knew all about Propter; he had engaged him in a conversation about Zen Buddhism. Desmond and one of the girls had moved the bottles, and were jiving. Vera was lying on the bed, a dreamy look on her face. Hoffmann occasionally looked at her with tired, hurt eyes; from Doreen's story, I understood the reason. I felt sorry for Hoffmann. He seemed even more out of place in the room than Propter. (Propter looked as if he were thoroughly enjoying himself.) Hoffmann was making a fool of himself about Vera, and he knew it. The girl was evidently a nymphomaniac, and he was attracted by some element of self-destruction in her. It was obvious that she would never take him seriously. It was not simply that he was twenty-five years her senior; he belonged to a more nervous, more sensitive generation, a generation which felt kinship with the Goncourt brothers, and were uninhibited about their frustrations and failures. If frustration was not a preoccupation of people like Vera and Tommy, it was because they never wanted anything long enough to get frustrated. This certainly constituted no superiority: yet I somehow preferred the Veras and Tommys. I preferred them in the way that Whitman preferred animals to human beings.

The record came to an end. Propter was asking Robby if he could see some of his poetry. I was glad that his visit had been of use to somebody. I called over to James (who had cornered a bottle of burgundy) to ask if we should take Sir Reginald up to see Ricky Prelati. Vera roused herself sufficiently to say: 'He's in one of his anti-social moods today. Says he's painting the mansions of eternal peace. He'll probably throw you out.'

'We'll try him, anyway,' James said. 'Will you come on up, Sir Reg?'

I went out of the room first. Doreen followed. I knocked on the door. No one answered. I opened it cautiously, afraid of being greeted by the same roar that had met me this morning. But Ricky was standing six feet away from his easel, staring at the painting. He seemed hypnotised. When I got into the room, I realised he had a model. A small, brown Hindu was squatting, quite naked, in the middle of the rug, his legs crossed. He also continued to stare blankly in front of him without moving a muscle. It was like walking into a waxworks. James and Sir Reginald followed us in. James was not at all disconcerted. He said: 'Ah, the master is in *samadhi*.'

He went and stood beside Ricky, and stared at his painting. After a moment, I went over too. I could see then why Ricky looked hypnotised. The painting was an incredible, abstract-looking effort, that might have been a luminous white jellyfish trailing nerve-like antennae through black water lit with red and yellow lights. But the white blob in the middle of the canvas concentrated the attention; everything seemed to lead back to it. After staring at it for a moment, I began to feel hypnotised myself.

James clapped Ricky on the back, saying: 'Master, you've produced a masterpiece. Don't you think so, Sir Reg?'

Ricky seemed to come out of his trance. He looked at us curiously, but without hostility, wondering how we got there. Propter said: 'A most remarkable work — most remarkable. Er... what do you call it?'

Ricky pointed to the naked Hindu. 'It's Narendra.'

Sir Reginald glanced at Narendra as if he might turn out to be the Thing from Outer Space. James introduced Propter to Ricky; they shook hands.

143

Propter said: 'Tell me, sir, would you consider selling that painting?'

Ricky shook his head vaguely. 'Oh no. No.'

We waited for further explanation, but none came. James interposed tactfully: 'It's not finished.'

Propter began to wander round the room. James obligingly turned on the spotlights and directed them at the pictures. I could see that Propter was as impressed as I had been that morning. He asked: 'Have you had any exhibitions?'

Ricky shook his head. He was still staring at the painting. At last he took up his palette again and added more paint. He said finally: 'I've only been painting for five years.'

'Indeed. What did you do before that?'

'Built bridges.'

'These are really quite astounding,' Propter said. He turned to James. 'I'm very grateful to you for bringing me here.'

James came over to him, and spoke in a low voice. Since I was standing next to them, I could just over-hear.

'Don't ask him about buying them now. He hates to sell his pictures. Wait until you know him better.'

I couldn't help admiring James's knack of creating 'sales interest'. Propter nodded briefly, and then contented himself with examining the painting without speaking. I noticed that Doreen was looking at Ricky with more interest than at the paintings, and felt a flash of jealousy. In the glare of the spotlights he was one of the most impressive-looking men I have seen. Between the domed, bald forehead and the black beard, the face showed power and character; but it also made an immediate impression of decency and good humour. I realised that I could hardly blame Doreen if she preferred him to me.

The door was suddenly flung open, and a tall, bearded man strode in. He was in evening clothes, and, unlike the rest of us (except Propter), was most aggressively well-dressed; from his carefully trimmed black beard to his glossy patent leather shoes, he looked as if a regiment of tailors had been at work on him. He said in a deep, pleasant voice: 'Aha, the master is at work, I see. Out of self-defence, no doubt?' I felt this last remark was pointed at us, but before I could feel offended, he went on: 'My God, if it isn't Reggie Propter! How are you, Reggie boy?'

Propter looked curiously embarrassed. I noticed that our satanic friend had been followed into the room by a slight, languid looking young man, also well-dressed in a fawn whipcord suit, with a silk choker under his shirt. When he saw James he smiled, fluttered his eyelids, and said: 'Hello, James dear. How nice to see you. Have you found yourself a rich heiress yet?'

'Nothing over sixty. I couldn't accept anything younger — not with death duties so high.'

The young man caught my eye, and wiggled his eyebrow at me. He said: 'I can see James doesn't intend to introduce us. I'm Eric Primrose.'

I shook hands with him, and had to repress a start as he tickled the palm of my hand with his forefinger. He said: 'You haven't met my friend Oswald Blichstein, have you?'

Blichstein acknowledged me with a courtly gesture that was like a half-bow. Then his eye fell on Ricky's new painting, and he drew himself up to his full height and waved his cane in the air.

'My God, master, you've achieved it at last! The power of Van Gogh, the structure of Cezanne, the mysticism of Simeon Solomon and the eroticism of de Sade! What a combination!'

Eric had wandered over to the little Hindu, who was still staring blankly into space. He looked down at him for a moment, then said: 'Hello, O sage. Are you still wandering around in the absolute? What's it like up there? Do the men wear clothes?' He said to Ricky, 'I don't know how you sleep at night with that lovely brown body in the room. Would he come round if you tried to roll him on his tummy?'

Blichstein said: 'Cockroach! You'd be struck down by Shiva!'

Ricky suddenly said, in a tired voice: 'Gentlemen, delightful as I find your company, I want to get on with some work. So could you come and see me some other time?'

'We were about to go,' Blichstein said. 'I just came in to tell you that a friend of mine wants you to do some work for him. He wants some obscene murals on the walls of his basement flat. He's a little man who worships the devil in a big way. Can you do it?'

'What's his name?' Ricky asked.

'Otto Roehmer. I think you know him.'

'Can he pay?'

'Certainly. He's stinking with money.'

'All right. Tell him to come and see me.'

Propter had been looking dubious during this exchange; now he said: 'Surely you don't have to do that kind of thing for money? I'd happily buy some of your paintings.'

'That's kind of you,' Ricky said. He sounded tired and uninterested. 'But I'd rather do hack work. I don't care to sell work I like.'

'But what *kind* of thing does this... devil worshipper expect you to paint.'

'Something he can wash with warm water,' Blichstein said languidly. 'They'll probably get smeared with cowdung in the priapic revels.'

James said insincerely: 'What about posterity, dear boy?'

146

'I prefer money,' Ricky said drily.

'Good man!' Blichstein shouted ecstatically. 'Serve ye Mammon with all thy heart and all thy soul and all thy libidinal energies.'

Propter looked nettled. He asked testily:

'Don't you think all that kind of thing's a bit old-fashioned, Blichstein?'

Blichstein assumed a puzzled and concerned expression. (He had the mobile face of an actor.)

'You worry me sometimes, Reggie. You change the subject in the oddest way. I knew a lunatic who was just like that. He went and joined moral rearmament. They didn't seem to notice when he was being irrelevant.'

'I merely commented that all this devil worship stuff is old-fashioned.'

'What has fashion got to do with it? Look at Eric. His sins are as old as Sodom. Would you condemn him for lacking originality?'

'I wish you'd leave me out of it,' Eric said. 'Why don't you go and commit some sins yourself? You're always talking about sin and crime, but you never commit any.'

'*E perchè*? The only real crimes are committed by space, time and chance, and we can never do them as much harm as they can do us.'

Doreen had been watching Blichstein with fascination. She asked: 'Are you really a devil worshipper?'

'I've no idea. I don't quite see how one can worship anything one hasn't met. I can easily worship young girls, or even attractive boys. But how does one worship God or the devil? You'd feel rather silly if someone proved conclusively they don't exist.'

Ricky said suddenly: 'I can paint things that don't exist.'

'Of course. Because you create them by painting them. If these religious people would admit that they create God by worshipping him, I wouldn't mind.'

I interposed: 'What about your devil worshipper friend? Does *he* really worship the devil?'

'I don't think so, although I was never curious enough to find out. He probably feels as I do — that life is basically rather absurd. The forces of destiny are inscrutable. The only certain thing is that they want us to behave like human beings. Unfortunately, I'm quite certain that I'm not a human being.'

'I always suspected it,' James murmured.

'I feel like a man who wakes up one morning and finds himself dressed in a monkey's skin. I resent being told I'm human. I'm certain it's all a confidence trick. I feel one's life ought to be a continual act of protest against the imposture. I stand for the abolition of humanity.'

'In that case, you should have joined Hitler's storm troopers,' Propter said.

'You fail to understand me. I don't speak of the inhuman, or even of the superhuman. I think our young friend here understands what I mean.'

He was talking about me. And I saw exactly what he meant. I said: 'I can see what you mean about destiny being inscrutable. I sometimes get such a strong feeling that somebody's playing a game with me that I want to turn round and shout, "Oi, come off it." I once played with an earwig and a piece of straw. Every time the earwig tried to walk away, I shifted the straw in front of it. Finally, I began to wonder why the earwig didn't look up at me and say, "What's the game?". I sometimes wonder if God feels the same way about human beings.'

'Precisely. No sensitive human being can believe that his fate's a matter of the immutable laws of nature. It's all *much* too personal.'

Eric said unexpectedly: 'Well, I wish you'd hurry up and find out. It'd be rather nice to be able to write letters to God complaining about the weather.'

'An interesting idea,' Propter said musingly. 'The decline of religion with the rise of democracy. Once upon a time you had to pray to God if you wanted something badly or had something to complain about. Nobody else was interested. And all misfortunes were acts of God. Then we got democracy, and people discovered they could write letters to *The Times* or their Member of Parliament. And we discover that nearly everything can be blamed on somebody.'

'And a very good thing too,' Eric said.

'Is it? You'd suppose that men would become more self-confident and sure of themselves. Instead, we live in an age of neurotics.'

'What does Hans Castorp have to say about that?' Blichstein said, smiling at me.

I looked from him to Propter, and saw why he was smiling. I stood between the two of them like Mann's ingénue between Settembrini and Naphta; on the one hand, humanism and common sense; on the other, anti-humanism and irrationality. In a way, my sympathies were all with Blichstein; but he seemed too histrionic to make a deep appeal to me.

'I see your point,' I said. 'When you say you stand for the abolition of humanity, you mean humanity in the sense of Nietzsche's "human all too human". It's a synonym for weakness and slavery. So you stand for metaphysical freedom.'

Blichstein grinned at Propter. 'Our young friend has a precise and logical mind.'

I went on, determined to get it said before he flattered me into concealing my misgivings: 'But I don't see your point about refusing to be human. I came to London because I wanted to find a kind of freedom. But I don't think I shall find it around Soho. For me, that's not freedom — it's only the appearance of freedom.' I felt it was James I was criticising, so I addressed myself to him. 'This kind of life — hanging around Soho cafés and sleeping on floors — doesn't satisfy me. I don't think that the answer *is* to find a new way of life. The way you live isn't the same thing as living.'

'My dear boy...' Blichstein began, when Ricky interrupted: 'Gentlemen, I find all this fascinating, but I have work to do. Why don't you go and smoke some hashish in the department below, or visit the sex department in the basement?'

'True!' Blichstein said. 'We interrupt the master. We should take our symposium elsewhere.'

But Propter wanted to ask Ricky about selling his painting and arranging an exhibition, and Eric seemed to be in the middle of an argument with James in which he declared that all great men of genius have been homosexual, and cited the usual list — Michelangelo, Leonardo, Plato, Shakespeare, Schubert, Beethoven. He even added Van Gogh, explaining that Van Gogh had cut off his ear because of his frustrated love for Gauguin. I beckoned to Doreen, and we sneaked out of the room. Blichstein came out after us on to the landing and gave me his card, making me promise to ring him at his address in Brook Street. I caught a look of disapproval on Doreen's face. As soon as Blichstein had gone back into the room, I asked what she thought of him.

'He's fascinating. But I don't think you ought to get too involved.'

'Why not?'

'Oh, I don't know. Do you think he's homosexual?'

'He might be. Not entirely, though. He looked at you like a man who knows what women are for.'

We went back into the room downstairs. I whispered, as we entered: 'Anyway, he won't lead me astray so long as I've got you.' To my delight, she pressed my hand.

Things were much as we had left them in the room below, except that the wine had disappeared, and the whisky was seriously depleted. I hastily helped myself to a large dose, to forestall the coming famine, and drank half of it quickly, by way of catching up. Hoffmann came over and asked me if I would like some tea; I said vaguely that it would be a nice idea, if there was any. He called to Vera: 'One more'll come in.' Doreen was seized by a thin, bearded man whom I had not met, and they began to dance to Brubeck. Doreen was no expert at jiving, but she had a graceful, sinuous way of moving that passed for skill. I saw Robby Dysart sitting forlornly in a corner, scribbling on a Woolworth's notepad, so I made my way over to him. He glanced at me, smiled, and went on writing. He began to chew the end of his pencil, frowning at the paper. Finally, he showed me what he had written. In a neat, perfectly legible hand, it read:

> 'I see they are uncertain, wild,
> Yet have not even
> Consistency of terror, changing
> To smiles and talk of heaven.
> Yet I am quiet as a murdered child
> Thin as a wraith, yet know
> One purpose, slight as spider's silk
> And that at least shall be fulfilled
> Though...'

'Difficult,' Robby said. 'I need a good last line. Something that really ties it up. How about "Though God himself said No"?'

I shook my head. It sounded wrong.

'Or "Though Hell's gusts blow"?'

It still sounded wrong. I ran through the rhymes to 'know'. Snow, blow, go, no, poe.

'How about "When I get the dough"?' I suggested.

He took this quite seriously, looked at the poem for a

moment, then shook his head: 'No, it won't fit.'

'Or "Come on, let's go", or "You said it, Joe".'

'I don't want it to sound like Auden,' he said.

I gave up my feeble attempts at humour.

At this moment Vera came over and said: 'You owe me five bob.'

'What for?' I asked.

'Tea. Come on in the other room.'

She went out. Robby said: 'You smoke tea, do you?'

I began to understand.

'What did she mean by tea?'

'Marijuana — hashish. Do you like it?'

I didn't like to admit that I had never tried it, so I only said: 'I don't make a habit of it.'

'I sometimes write better on tea,' Robby said. 'I wonder if I could have a drag of yours?'

'Certainly,' I said cordially. 'I'll bring it in.'

'No, you can't do that. We can be seen from the windows of the opposite flat. I'll come in there.'

We went into the other part of the room — the annexe — which could not be seen from the window. Vera and Hoffmann were sitting on a bed, shredding a packet of cigarettes on a newspaper. They mixed the heap of tobacco with a grey-green powder, then re-rolled the cigarettes, this time in a brown cigar paper. I was handed one of these brown cigarettes. I held it out to Robby, but he said politely: 'No, it's your five bob.' This reminded me to produce my money. I took my time over it, being unwilling to light up first. Desmond and a girl drifted in. They insisted on rolling their own cigarette, and putting a double helping in it. The result was a fat and stubby cigar. By this time I could put it off no longer, so I sat on the bed and struck a match. The first mouthful tasted like any other cigarette — slightly hotter, perhaps, but with no startling effects. I noticed Hoffmann eyeing me with ironical disdain; no doubt he recognised my inexperience. So I took an enormous mouthful, and inhaled it ostentatiously. In a few moments I was high. I took another couple of draws, and handed it to Robby (noticing, to my disgust, that the cigarette had already half burnt away). There was a sensation like rising very fast in a lift, and nothing seemed to matter. I could understand why they insisted on smoking the stuff in the other room. I had supposed that an observer from the flats across the way would hardly be able to recognise hashish at fifty yards' distance. But it was not so simple as recognition of the cigarettes; I wanted to sink into a pose of utter abandonment, and then embrace the world, and any trained observer could recognise the symptoms. I relaxed on the bed and stretched myself; I felt like a Persian cat, Vera had also lit up by this time. I caught her eye and smiled; she seemed like a combination of sister and wife. She came and lay on the bed, shifted her weight on to me, and pressed her mouth to mine. Five minutes before my immediate reaction would have been to look around for Doreen; now I didn't care. I kissed her back, and let my hands caress the small buttocks in the tight jeans. It was not that I felt sexually excited by Vera. Since I had seen her in bed with two men, I felt strangely prudish about her. But she seemed a warm and delicious human being, and the world was full of decent and infinitely lovable people. So I kissed her back, and ran my fingers through her rather coarse black hair. Then she unwound herself from me, and I saw Doreen standing by the bed. She looked amused. I sat up, and said, slowly and steadily: 'I am expressing the brotherhood of all men.'

'Are you drunk?' she asked, with no more than mild curiosity.

Robby handed me back the cigarette. There was about a quarter left. I held it out to Doreen: 'Try it.'

'What is it?'

'Tea.'

She looked at it, then at me, then, very slowly, took it and raised it to her mouth.

'Inhale,' I said.

She did.

'Isn't it splendid?' I asked.

She nodded. 'Rather nice.'

Hoffmann and Vera were now locked in an embrace. I wanted to say, 'Hoffmann, you have a splendid name', but it seemed too much trouble. Then I realised that the cigarette had burned down to my fingers. I dropped it on the floor, stamped it out, and went in search of my whisky glass. I was not drunk, but the drug had completed the work of the alcohol, and I felt liberated.

But before I could cross the room — avoiding a dancing couple — I felt the ominous lurch in the stomach that warned me I was going to have trouble. The room felt stuffy. I wandered into the kitchenette, and, to my relief, found a box of sodium bicarbonate. I dissolved a quantity of this in water and drank it down. This made me feel better, but it reduced the effect of the marijuana. I opened the window wide, and leaned out into the night. The wind was cold. From somewhere nearby I could hear music — someone was playing the prelude to *Rheingold* with the window wide open. From where I was leaning I could see the lighted window of the room next door, and the jiving figures; but the jazz was hardly audible. I realised what Oswald Blichstein meant when he said life was absurd. These figures were human beings enjoying themselves and forgetting the strange and paradoxical destiny of man. Yet through the glass they were parodies of people, like the distorted sketches of Toulouse Lautrec, who must have seen the Moulin Rouge as I now saw the room next door. All motion was absurd — except perhaps the motion of a pen across a sheet of paper, the silent motion of Balzac concentrated on a great design. The poet of Shakespeare's atrocious lines, his 'eye in fine frenzy rolling', could never exist — except, perhaps, played by some ham in a provincial touring company. The artist is a kind of spider.

The marijuana intoxication had subsided, leaving only a slight disgust. The kind of muzzy happiness it created was the enemy of incisive thought or feeling. Even wine deadened the perception of the world's curious combination of treachery and loveliness. I pushed my fingers down my throat, and deliberately made myself sick in the sink. Then I turned on the tap, and used a bottle brush to remove the splashes from the tiles under the taps. The contents of my stomach were less acidic than I had anticipated; my teeth still felt smooth afterwards, and had not acquired a ground-glass surface. I washed out my mouth, and went downstairs.

I unlocked Doreen's door and crossed to the bed without switching on the light. The fire had been switched off, and the room was pleasantly cold. I also felt cold — but not physically. I sat on the bed and stared at the lamplight on the opposite wall, and the shadows of the branches of the tree, and listened to the ticking of a clock that came from Doreen's open case, still on the bed.

About half-an-hour later she came down and switched on the light. She asked: 'Are you all right?'

'Yes, thanks. Are you?'

'I'm very tired.'

'How did the marijuana effect you?'

'Not very much. It made things go in slow motion. How about you?'

'It affected me more than that. But it's worn off now.'

'Had you smoked it before?'

'No.'

'I don't think it's very good for you. Don't let it become a habit, will you?'

I said, smiling: 'Don't worry. I don't think I shall ever touch the stuff again.'

She looked curious, but I didn't enlighten her. I stood up.

'You want to come to bed. Do you want me to sleep upstairs?'

A touch of mockery appeared in her smile. 'Why? Do you want to sleep with Vera?'

I said, with astonishment: 'Good heavens, no! Not in the least.'

It was obvious she did not believe me. Recalling my position on the bed with Vera, I could not blame her. She moved the suitcase, stripped the bed, and made it up with sheets, while I sat at the table and stared at the pattern formed by a pool of tea and some floating tea-leaves on the plastic cloth. There was a definite significance in it, like a well-drawn geometric illustration. Then Doreen went out of the room. She said over her shoulder: 'You can sleep where you like.'

I needed no encouragement. Within half-a-minute I was between her cold sheets, inhaling the scent of her hair on the pillow. But I felt no kind of desire to make love to her. An hour later I woke up and found her beside me, wearing a woollen bed jacket over the nylon nightdress. But she was breathing quietly, her face turned to the ceiling. I put my hand on her waist, and fell asleep again.

Part 2

Chapter One

So far, I have been able to tell of the events of my first few days in London without any break in sequence. This has been easy; the days were so crowded that, even as it is, I have been forced to select carefully when deciding what to record. But as soon as I began to share a room with Doreen the pace slackened; I took good care that it should. It was also at about this time that James was offered a job in pantomime at Luton, so for a few weeks I saw little of him. In some ways this was a relief; I felt that Doreen regarded his influence uneasily.

At this point, I should say something about Doreen. Until we moved into the Ladbroke Road house I can hardly claim that I knew her. My experience of women had not been wide. Doreen bowled me over. I could hardly believe my luck. For years I had been telling myself that the price you paid for being a poet and philosopher was a certain incompetence in the affairs of the world. Discipline amounted to a starvation of the human appetites. And yet Doreen seemed to accept me with a confidence she did not show towards James or any of the crowd upstairs. It took me some time to realise this; and it only sank home as I came to understand something of Doreen's character.

Her father was a man with a strong temper, and a roving eye for women; he was the head buyer of a chain of stores in New Zealand. Doreen had three elder brothers, all of whom fought violently with her father. She was his favourite; yet his temper was so uncontrolled that she was afraid of him. Later, when she came to realise that he kept several mistresses, she began to resent him too. She was particularly incensed by his preference for Maori girls. Her mother, a pale, placid woman, took his infidelities for granted, and amused herself by giving music classes for the Workers' Educational Association. Doreen began to take part-time music classes at Canterbury University College, Christchurch, where she allowed a piano teacher of twice her age to convince her that she was in love with him. He was, apparently, thin, balding and with a tendency to consumption, and his wife was a virago. He wanted to marry Doreen, but was afraid of the effect of scandal on his university post; so he took rooms in another part of the town, and tried to persuade Doreen to move in as his mistress. Fortunately, before she made up her mind, her father got wind of the affair, told the professor's wife, and threatened the professor with a revolver. The wife apparently felt no special concern about her husband's job; by way of punishing him, she spread the scandal all over Christchurch. Doreen's father bundled her off to England and told her he would make her an allowance for six months. She had been in England about a week when I met her.

As I came to know her, I realised that she was an easygoing, sweet-tempered and rather weak girl. Men of strong character and obvious Don Juans frightened her. She had no real understanding of music or capacity for ideas, but her mother had convinced her that both should be held in respect. She was also a lonely girl, who badly needed companionship, and would accept it at almost any price (hence her acquaintance with the sporty type). I came to realise later that I suited her perfectly. I was the opposite of her father, and I brought her into contact with a houseful of interesting people, while serving as a protection against too much contact.

James would no doubt have been ironically amused if he had known that I continued to sleep with her without becoming, in the technical sense, her lover. The music master had not seduced her, and I was too happy at being allowed in the same bed with her to try to force her. She was by no means frigid; up to a point it was obvious that she derived enormous pleasure from physical contact; beyond that point she was like a sleepwalker suddenly awakened on the edge of a cliff.

My own feelings for her went through several stages. My previous relations with women had ended in humiliation or frustration. Consequently, my first response to her was a controlled admiration — the kind we feel towards an object we know to be beyond our means. The afternoon I spent in her flat altered this; she seemed a mother-figure, a kind of protecting angel. At the same time she was a pretty and sexually desirable girl; sleeping in her bed, having to move the drying rack with her underwear out of the bath, using her bath salts — all these things intoxicated me; they were contact with a mystery. I could recognise my feelings in Goethe's lyrics to Frederike and Charlotte. Yet here I made a discovery. I had never been able to understand how Goethe had been able to desert Frederike, how his love for her was not absolute. Now I realised that my feeling for Doreen had all the quality of complete infatuation; yet it was not a desire to marry her, to bind her to me permanently. I suppose my attitude could be defined by saying that, since the fates had shown themselves so well-disposed towards me, there would be no sense in obstructing their future generosity by mortgaging myself.

Besides, there were still further changes in my feelings. Close contact with Doreen did not encourage a romantic mystique. She certainly had no tendency to regard herself as an embodiment of the eternal feminine; there was no attempt to make a mystery of herself. Various personal items that a Victorian girl

161

would die rather than mention were left around the room or on the bed, even when visitors came into the room. After our second night together, she dressed and undressed in front of me without shame; she would even stand naked on the rug, after a bath, and dry herself in front of the electric fire. This certainly had not the effect of making me less attached to her; but it made it impossible to maintain the completely romantic attitude to which I am so prone.

During my first few days in the room, the situation seemed a delicate one. I was afraid that Doreen might feel I was simply moving in on her. It was her room, after all. It would have been easy to suggest that I should share the rent, but that might have made her feel that she had to make a decision. I suppose I could have bought myself a cheap camp-bed in the Portobello Road, and slept with the others upstairs; but I needed a certain amount of privacy. Besides, Doreen might think it was an excuse to sleep with Vera or one of the other female casuals. I decided to ask Ricky Prelati if he had another spare room. I went up early one morning and caught him washing at the kitchen sink, lathering his huge, hairy chest with carbolic soap.

'Can't really help you much,' he said, when I had explained my problem. 'There's that room over there, but it's sort of occupied.' He nodded to the room across the landing, which I had assumed to be the lavatory. 'Haven't seen the bloke for a few weeks, but his rent's paid up for another couple of months.'

'If he hasn't been back, he must have another place,' I suggested.

'Not necessarily. He's an odd bloke — sort of student of yoga. He told me he once went into a trance on the Circle line and stayed on the train for two days.'

He showed me the room. It was — as I had thought — a disused lavatory and bathroom, about five feet by ten. There was no bath in it, but there was a lavatory stool that was not connected to the water supply. Someone had covered this over with a tea chest, and used the chest as a table. There was no furniture in the room, only two old army blankets in a corner, on the bare floorboards. A shelf erected about six feet off the ground seemed to contain a few personal odds and ends.

'I only charge him five bob a week for it,' Ricky said. 'Next time he turns up, I'll ask him if he still wants it.'

The room seemed ideal for my needs. I could move a camp bed in there, and keep it as a subsidiary bedroom. Doreen might then cease to feel that she was landed with me. I found it hard to contain my impatience about the fool who occupied it at present. But there was nothing to be done. So I went off to the British Museum for the day, so that Doreen would have the room to herself. On the way there, I brooded about my situation. In almost every way I was better off than I had been in my home town; I had been incredibly lucky to meet James, and then find this place. But there was still the problem of supporting myself. I decided to find out all I could about the community upstairs. But the fact remained that I needed a basically ordered life. James's ingenious methods of avoiding work cost more energy than a straightforward job.

This came home to me even more forcibly when I got into the Reading Room. I had decided to begin making notes for my volume on the nature of freedom. I intended to make the book a contrast between two ideals of freedom — the religious ideal and the social ideal. In the first part I wanted to write about all the religious preachers of the end of the world and of a total change in the human condition; I would examine the Jewish idea of the Messiah, and all the post-Christian prophecies of a second coming. Certain German mystics of the fourteenth century believed that a new type of man was about to appear, who would be incapable of suffering — a man-god. But all the religious Utopians believed that there could be no human perfection until after the last judgement. In the second part of the volume I wanted to trace the growth of social ideals of freedom, beginning with More's *Utopia* and Campanella's *City of the Sun*. It would centre round Rousseau's 'Man is born free'.

But as soon as I found myself a seat in the Reading Room the desire to work disappeared. There were too many books around me, too many things I had always wanted to read. I ordered several volumes on the history of religions; but it was impossible to concentrate. I could not harness my excitement to the task of reading about the dating of the Old Testament. Instead, I found myself watching an attractive blonde girl who was searching in the subject catalogues. Then a girl in a tight pink cardigan came and sat next to me. She was not particularly pretty, but she was wearing some scent — or perhaps it was just a scented toilet soap — that I found disturbing. She reached up to turn on her reading lamp, and the cardigan came out of the top of the tweed skirt, revealing some pink flesh. I found myself wondering why she was not wearing a slip on a chilly December day. Then it struck me to reflect about my own curiosity; why should I feel the need for an insight into a life that, after all, was probably quite uninteresting? It was an impulse that had the same source as my inability to concentrate on the higher criticism when there were so many other books around me. It is not enough for the human consciousness to expand beyond its own narrow existence; it wants to penetrate simultaneously into every other existence in the universe. It is an irritating frame of mind, this, for it leads to frustration and boredom.

Failing total insight, the imagination falls into a kind of sulk, a refusal to content itself with the second best. But how, in that case, had men like Balzac and Zola managed to contain themselves, and work on one book at a time?

My own listlessness infuriated me, and the fury was just beginning to warm me into a mood of creation when I saw the blonde girl walking past, and found my eyes following her movements. How could I be expected to take any interest in the origins of Christianity when the problem of a girl's slip was so much more immediate? I closed my books and went outside. It was raining. To try to defeat the boredom, which was invading my whole body, I walked out in the rain. In a few minutes I was soaked. I turned towards Tottenham Court Road, and found myself outside Major Noyes's house. I decided to go up and have a look round. The dusty-looking woman was still half-hidden behind the shelves. The only other person in the room was a ragged looking man in a filthy raincoat. He had a beard that looked like a bird's nest, and he smelt distinctly of sweat. As I stood next to him, he snuffled loudly and wiped his nose on the sleeve of his raincoat. I glanced at the book in his hands, and saw that it was printed in a symbolism I did not recognise (it was actually Hebrew). I found a cheap copy of Reinach's *Orpheus,* and was about to pay the dusty-looking woman when the Major came in. I don't think he recognised me, but I said hello, and he stopped and held out his hand.

'Ah, it's you! How are you?'

Then he saw the raincoated man. His expression became more cautious. He said in a colder voice: 'Hello, Danvers. We haven't seen you for a long time.'

'No, I've been in the country.' He spoke with a Welsh accent, and his voice was infinitely more pleasant than his appearance; in fact, it was one of those sweet, Celtic voices that seem designed to charm.

'Nice to see you again,' the major said, and slapped me on the shoulder as he headed for the door that led to his cubbyhole. Then, by way of making his departure less abrupt, he asked me: 'Have you two met? No? This is Danvers Reed. Danvers, er...'

I could see he had forgotten my name, so I hastily supplied it. The Welshman nodded at me, and a dewdrop on the end of his nose vibrated. The Major asked him: 'Still living in that lavatory?' and without waiting for a reply vanished through his door. The Welshman turned back to his book.

It took a few minutes for the major's final remark to make an impression on me. When it did, I said diffidently: 'Excuse me...'

He turned his watery grey eyes on me. With his runny nose and uncombed beard, his face looked like a badly made fruit gateau that is beginning to turn into a sodden mass. I said: 'Excuse my asking, but... whereabouts is the — er — lavatory that Major Noyes referred to?'

For a moment, I thought he was going to tell me to mind my own business. Then he told me. It was just as I had suspected. It was the place Ricky had shown me that morning. The coincidence seemed incredible. I explained that I had been looking at his room a few hours ago.

He asked politely: 'Indeed? And how is that?'

'I moved into the house a few days ago. I was talking to Ricky about letting me a room this morning, and he said he'd ask you if you wanted yours.'

'I don't understand. You moved in, but you say you haven't a room.'

I explained this briefly. He said finally: 'It was kind of Ricky to say he had to consult me. After all, it's his house.'

166

'But your rent is paid for another two months.'

'Is it? Good. I didn't know. Perhaps I'd better go and see him. How much rent did he say?'

'Two months, I think.'

'Mm. That would be about two pounds. I wonder if he'd be willing to refund the money?'

'I'll give you two pounds now, with pleasure,' I said. I could hardly believe my luck. I produced my wallet and took out the money. He said: 'Very well.' His hand was trembling as he took the money. Then he turned to the flyleaf of the book he was reading, and handed it to the dusty-looking woman.

'Ten shillings, I believe. Don't you think the Major might reduce the price a little? After all, nobody reads Hebrew nowadays.'

She stared at him stonily, without speaking, as if she felt too much contempt even to express her refusal. Then she went into the next room and returned with a ten shilling note and a florin. I noticed the kindly gleam in her eyes; it looked out of place in that parchment face. The Welshman said courteously: 'I thank you, madame.'

I paid for my book and left. I was frozen; rain had trickled from my wet hair and down my back. But I could hardly walk away without thanking the Welshman. He was standing in the doorway, looking at the rain. I asked him if he would care to come and have a drink.

'I never drink beer. Disgusting drink.'

'I... thought of having some hot grog. It's rather chilly.'

'Ah. That's different. Then perhaps you will allow me to change my mind.'

We went to a pub near the Museum. The barman looked at my companion without approval. However, he went off to get us hot rum with lemon. As the

Welshman sat down the front of his raincoat opened slightly, and I realised that he was wearing no shirt underneath it. He sat staring in front of him, making no attempt to open a conversation. The barman brought our drinks, and I ordered a ham sandwich. I asked the Welshman if he would like a sandwich, but he only shook his head. I watched him stirring the sugar into his rum, using a ball point pen. Then he took a sip, and an expression of almost religious ecstasy came over his face. He looked as if he were about to faint. He took several deep gulps. (When I tasted my own, I could only just manage to sip it without it scalding my tongue.) By way of opening a conversation, I asked him where he was living at present. He stared at me uncomprehendingly, and finally said: 'In London.' He finished the rum, and I asked him if he would have another. He nodded, and I went over to the counter and ordered it. When it came, a few minutes later, he pushed a florin towards me.

'I can't have you paying for my drinks. Haven't you had another?'

I said I didn't want a second. He added: 'I had to let you order it. He wants to throw me out.' (nodding towards the barman). I glanced at the barman's face, and had to admit that the Welshman had probably read his thoughts correctly.

Halfway through his second rum, he seemed to expand. The colour came to his cheeks. Suddenly he laid his hand on my arm, and said: 'It's kind of you to put up with a beggarly fellow like me.'

I said that he didn't strike me as looking particularly beggarly. I said it out of politeness, and he seemed to know this.

'Of course I look like a beggar,' he said, in a tone of invincible certainty. 'It's not at all difficult. Anybody can do it.'

'I suppose so,' I said dubiously. I stopped talking while I ate my sandwiches. He produced a handkerchief and blew his nose — a concession, I think, to my appetite. He began to ask me questions about myself, and I told him, between mouthfuls, about my book on freedom. (I was in that early stage of the book when I was happy to talk about it to anybody.) At once I saw that I had his interest. He edged over closer to me, and leaned across the table. (This was not a pleasing development; the hot rum made him sweat heavily, and his mingled odours rose with the steam of his body until I thought I was sitting next to a manure heap.) I hastily swallowed the last mouthful and washed it down with grog. Some mention I had made of Suso or Tauler sent him off into a kind of daydream. His watery eyes stared blankly; he blinked, and the tears ran down his cheeks, but he was so concentrated on his thoughts that he was unaware of them.

In my embarrassment, I turned to the barman and asked for two more rums. The Welshman came back to consciousness, and said: 'No, not for me. Two is fine. It makes me feel good. It relaxes and fills the body with well-being. Three would make me stupid.' So I had to call to the barman to cancel one of them. This was one more than I had intended to drink. But, in my delight at getting his room, I felt that a little excess might be allowed.

When I went to the bar to collect it, the barman nodded to someone in the next bar, and a grey-moustached little man came through. He beckoned me closer and leaned over the counter to me, then said quietly: 'Don't think I want to be awkward, but this place is going to fill up with the lunch hour customers in another ten minutes, and your friend there...' He stopped, looking embarrassed. 'Do you see what I mean?'

'Don't worry. We're going now.'

He said quickly: 'I don't want you to feel you're being thrown out. You're not. I leave it to your own discretion. But you see my point, don't you?' He nodded towards the Welshman. Noticing that my friend showed no reaction, and was staring into space again, he went on, in a louder voice: 'I don't mind who comes in here, myself. If a navvy wants to drink in his shirt-sleeves, I'm not going to tell him he's got to wear a suit. But if the other customers stop coming in because they don't like it, I've got my business to protect, haven't I?'

I could see he was a decent little man who was genuinely concerned about having to ask us to go. So I assured him that I could understand his viewpoint, and took a gulp of my grog. He said anxiously: 'You needn't hurry. In your own good time...'

I went back and sat down. The Welshman didn't even bother to ask me what I'd been saying. I doubt whether he noticed. I had poured a little cold water into my drink, and swallowed it quickly.

He said immediately: 'Let me buy you another.'

'No, really. I couldn't drink it.'

'Yes... you've bought me one. Let me buy you another.'

He actually got up to go to the counter. I held him back by the sleeve. I said: 'As a matter of fact, I don't think they want us to stay.'

He shrugged, turned, and walked towards the door. I followed him out, feeling ashamed of myself for making the admission. But I could think of no other way of stopping him.

I could also think of nothing to say that wouldn't make it worse. We walked in the direction of the Museum. Finally I said: 'I don't think they meant to be offensive. But he said the lunch hour crowd...'

He interrupted me: 'You don't have to tell me. I'm not offended.'

We turned into the Museum gates and crossed the courtyard.

'Are you coming in?' I asked him.

He looked at me and grinned. He obviously thought I was worried in case the pub incident was repeated in the Museum; in this he was wrong. He said: 'No. I shall sit outside for a few minutes.'

We sat on the bench where I had sat with de Bruyn two days before. He picked up a matchstick off the ground, gnawed the end between his teeth, and began to poke about under his filthy nails. I couldn't help feeling it was a little late to start bothering about his toilet. He said musingly: 'Some people dress like beggars because they don't know any better. Others lack the will-power to keep themselves clean. I dress like a beggar because I prefer to.'

Since he was being candid, and I still felt a kind of resentment towards him since the pub incident, I asked bluntly: 'Why?'

He noticed my tone, and smiled.

'One of the first things I ever noticed about people is that they're completely contemptible. When I was a young man, I wanted to commit suicide out of sheer disgust at belonging to the human race. There is no name to describe the malice and pettiness and stupidity of most people. Yet for some strange reason the basic human appetite is to think well of oneself. Is that not true? Everybody lusts after self-approval. Everybody wants to be admired and envied by his fellows. So what use is all the talk about salvation? Nobody wants to be saved. Everybody wants to feel important. So I made a vow that I'd try to save myself from lusting after the approval of fools. I never wash. I never change my clothes. In public, I always make a point of blowing my nose on my fingers and throwing the snot on the ground. This makes people hate me. So I'm never tempted to think well of my fellow men. When a man declares human beings are wonderful, he's either a liar or a self-deceiver.'

I found myself enormously impressed by his conviction. But certain aspects of what he said worried me. I said: 'But why do you dislike people so much?'

'You're mistaken. I don't dislike them. On the contrary, I love them. But I want to love them for what they really are. Did you ever read Peer Gynt? Do you remember the hall of the mountain kings, where the Trolds offer to believe all Peer's lies provided he'll believe theirs? That's human society for you. You should go and sit in the House of Commons some time. They're all in the conspiracy to take one another seriously. "Mr. Speaker, would the honourable member explain himself more fully?" Nobody's ever grown-up inside. Nobody's really self-confident. We're all terrified of one another and terrified to live. So we play games to reassure ourselves. And it's a temptation... to join in the game. You reassure me and I'll reassure you. There's only one way to stay detached. Make sure that you're an offence to human nostrils. Then nobody invites you to join in the game. Have you ever heard of Crates?'

I had to admit that I hadn't.

'He was the only completely honest philosopher the world has ever known. He was a follower of Diogenes and Bryson the Achaean. One day he gave away all his money and became a beggar. He just lived out of dustbins. Instead of washing, he rubbed himself up against walls when he got too filthy. He disapproved of Diogenes because Diogenes made a great show of hating people. Crates didn't hate people — he just didn't want to join in the game of make-believe. They

172

say his body was a mass of scabs. He made a special point of farting in public. A beautiful young girl insisted on becoming his mistress, and he told her she'd have to get used to eating out of dustbins and copulating in public, like dogs. As soon as his daughter grew up, he gave her to his disciples. He was one of the greatest men who ever lived.'

I was far from being convinced by all this, although his immense conviction was incredibly impressive. Half of what he said I agreed with; I wanted to be left alone to think it out and decide which of us was wrong about the other half. So I only asked non-committally: 'Where can I read about this bloke?'

'There's an account in Diogenes Laertius, and Marcel Schwob has a short story about him.'

He sat quietly, while I brooded about what he had said. I said finally: 'The trouble with living like this chap Crates is that it makes life so pointless. I think I prefer the stupidest money-grubbing bourgeois to a philosopher who insists on living like a dog. After all, why do human beings *want* life to have a meaning? It can't all be self-deception.'

'You're right, of course, to some extent. But you make the same mistake that you made five minutes ago. Then you asked me why I hated people, and I had to point out that I don't. Now you think I want life to be meaningless. I don't. I want it to alter completely. Everything has got to *change*.'

He ground out the word 'change' between his teeth. Then he stared gloomily at the pigeons that strutted near us. Suddenly he stood up. 'I shall go and look at the Egyptian mummies. Do you want to come?'

I felt, from his tone, that he wanted to be alone. So I made an excuse. He went off. I drifted back into the Reading Room, haunted by the tone of voice in which he had uttered that word 'change'. The girl next to me had gone for lunch. Her desk was now piled with volumes of Balzac in French. As I looked at these, I understood suddenly what the Welshman had meant by 'change'. This whole building was a monument to human achievement. Yet it was also a monument to a particular vision of humanity, and therefore a kind of gravestone of the whole human race. All man's errors, all his mistakes in his way of seeing himself, were enshrined here. Balzac might be regarded as a great creator. Or he might be regarded as the perpetuator of a stupid error about human nature. For human beings in his novels are creatures with definite contours and definite limitations. But supposing human beings aren't really in the least like that? Supposing they are really racehorses mistaking themselves for cows? Or even clouds mistaking themselves for mountains? Was there any limit to man's misunderstanding of his own nature?

I felt too excited to sit reading the higher criticism. So I handed the volumes in at the counter, put slips in them all so that I could come in the next day, and went home. I got off the tube at Holland Park, and walked along to the Portobello Road. I had noticed a camp bed in a junk shop a few days before, when Doreen and I had bought the other items. It was still there. One of its legs was cracked, but I decided it could be repaired with a piece of wood and some strong wire. So I handed over the seven-and-six, bundled it under my arm, and walked it home.

As soon as I got in, I dumped the bed in Doreen's room (she was out) and went upstairs to tell Ricky about my encounter with the Welshman. I knocked on his door. When there was no reply, I went in. The first thing I saw was a slender girl of about seventeen lying naked on the bed, her head propped up on the palm of her hand. I was about to apologise and back out when

Ricky looked round the canvas, and said: 'Oh, hello, Harry. Come in.'

I closed the door behind me. He went on painting. He glanced up to say: 'Have you met Melanie?'

The girl smiled at me, and said hello with a delicious French accent. Then she pouted at Ricky: 'My arm is getting tired. Can I have a rest?'

'You can get dressed now,' Ricky said. 'I'm going to work on the background.'

She bounced up like a rubber ball, and went to stand at the side of Ricky and look at the painting. My heart did a somersault. She had the loveliest body I had ever seen. (I should add that my acquaintance with naked seventeen-year-olds was neither wide nor deep.) She pulled a face, and asked: 'Is that mess supposed to be me?'

'It's much more important than you, my sweet,' Ricky said. 'You were only its inspiration.'

Melanie flounced off behind a screen, and started to dress.

'Melanie is your landlady's daughter,' Ricky told me.

'Is he living here?' Melanie asked.

'He's in the downstairs room.'

I took the opportunity to tell Ricky about meeting the Welshman.

'Good. So it's your room now. What did you think of Danvers?'

'A most extraordinary man,' I said.

'I cannot bear him,' Melanie said. '*Ca pue.*'

'He wants to stink,' Ricky said.

'I am glad he has left. He make me feel sick.' She eyed me with detachment. 'You look cleaner.'

'I should hope so,' I said.

She was wearing a fawn woollen dress that made her look almost as attractive dressed as undressed. She came over to me and, to my delight, pressed her small nose against my neck and sniffed.

'You don't stink either.'

It was hard to restrain an impulse to seize her and hug her. There was something about her that invited intimacy, like a fluffy kitten. I lowered my face to her black hair (which for some reason smelt of woodsmoke), and said: 'Neither do you.'

She smiled up at me and asked: 'You both want some tea?'

'Please.'

'Olright,' she said, and went out.

I drew in a deep breath, and said: 'She's the sort of girl I'd like to eat with Worcester sauce.'

'I know. She's an adorable little thing. She seems to find you attractive. Would Doreen object if you seduced her?'

'Probably. Why? Do you think she needs seducing?'

'I'm certain of it. She's always asking me if she can pose for me. Or cook me meals. Or make tea.'

'Where does she live?'

'With her mother, in Westbourne Grove. Five minutes away. Her mother owns this place.'

I sat down on a chair and watched Ricky paint. I could not agree with Melanie about his new picture. It was certainly not flattering to her, but it was as arresting as all his pictures. As I watched Ricky, I realised that I liked him immensely. He was a handsome man, and he probably had genius. And yet he was a man without any affectation or conceit. He was open and candid, and seemed immeasurably good tempered. As I sat there, it came to me that he was a man with every possible qualification for success, success on every level. I said: 'Don't you find Melanie attractive?'

Before he could answer, Melanie popped her head round the door. She said: 'Your milk has turned sour. I am going out to buy some.'

'Thank you, sweetheart,' Ricky said. We heard her footsteps descending the stair. I was about to repeat my question, when Ricky said: 'Of course I find her attractive. What sane man wouldn't? But she's not only attractive — she's completely inexperienced. She wants a love affair.'

'I'd find it hard to disoblige her.'

'So do I. But where would be the sense in it? I'm living in her mother's house. She's only five minutes away. She'd want to come and live here. Then I'd never get any work done.'

I was still shattered with the memory of her lovely naked body, and the feeling of her breath against my neck. I said: 'I don't think I could behave rationally.'

'*I* don't want to. But I know sex is an illusion. It's the most fascinating of all illusions. If I had time — or if I was a writer, like you — I'd spend my life studying it. But what's the point? In my situation, there are only two sensible things to do about sex. Find a nice, tractable girl, and marry her. Or go to bed with girls like Vera — girls who like having sex and aren't ashamed of liking it. But if I gave way to the urge to cuddle Melanie, she'd become violently possessive in twenty-four hours. I'd cease to have any private life.'

'I'm afraid you don't get much now,' I said.

'No. I get a lot of interruptions. That's where Melanie's useful — she keeps people away. Especially women.'

While Ricky was in a talkative mood, I decided to broach another matter that puzzled me.

'Don't mind me asking, but why don't you let some-body arrange an exhibition for you?'

'I'm not ready yet,' he said.

'I don't quite see that. I find your painting tremen-dously impressive. So did Sir Reginald Propter the other night. There's something very striking about

177

your painting. It's the sort of thing that could become fashionable in twenty-four hours. Not,' I hastened to add, 'that I think that's important. But you might just as well make money.'

'I agree. And, if I needed money, I'd try to sell pictures. But Melanie's mother lets me have this room free, in exchange for collecting her rents. I make a few pounds a week by doing woodcuts for a couple of galleries — I've even got a gallery in Paris that buys my woodcuts in quantity. So I'd rather learn how to paint.'

Melanie stuck her head round the door.

'You men are deaf. The kettle has been whistling for ten minutes.'

We apologised, and the subject of Ricky's painting was dropped. I could see what he meant. The paintings in the room showed an astonishing variety of style; they ranged from two dimensional abstracts that might have been painted by a disciple of Mondrian to paintings with a curiously violent technique, reminiscent of Van Gogh or Vlaminck. The canvases had only one thing in common — all had a vital sense of colour that made an immediate impact. Ricky could paint — there was no doubt about that; at the same time, I could understand what he meant when he said he was still learning to paint. He obviously had thousands of pictures in him; his main problem was to learn how to get them on to canvas in the best way. It was a self-completed circuit — from Ricky to the canvas. Where was the point of dragging in the public?

Melanie brought in the tray, then crossed to the window and closed it. Ricky said: 'Did I hear someone call my name?'

'Perhaps,' Melanie said sedately. Ricky tried to cross to the window, and she barred his way.

'You don't want to see people, no?'

'No,' Ricky agreed. Then he added curiously: 'Who is it — a woman?'

Melanie poured the tea, while Ricky tried to peer down towards the front door without making himself visible. He said: 'Why isn't the bell ringing?'

'Because I disconnect it,' Melanie said. She handed me my tea. Ricky raised his eyebrows and winked at me. 'I see her taxi arrive as I come in,' Melanie explained. 'So I bolt the door and disconnect the bell.'

'Taxi!' Ricky said. 'Who do I know who's rich enough to use taxis?'

As he spoke, we heard footsteps on the stairs, and for a moment Melanie looked like an angry kitten. Then she shrugged and cast her eyes up to the ceiling. The footsteps passed the first landing and came up the last flight. Melanie said: 'Your lady friends are very persistent.'

The door opened, and I saw why Melanie had disconnected the bell. The girl who came in was strikingly beautiful in a prima donna-ish way, and she looked like a woman who has money and knows how to use it with perfect taste. She was the sort of girl you see on the cover of *Harper's Bazaar*. For a moment she didn't see Melanie, who was behind a canvas.

She said: 'Ricky, darling!' and kissed him. Ricky squirmed (probably conscious of Melanie's murderous glare), and the woman deliberately prolonged the kiss, pulling his head down to her. Then she let him go, and saw Melanie. She said coolly: 'Oh hello dear. Are you modelling again?'

It was some of the most perfectly calculated bitchery I have ever seen, implying that Melanie was there as a kind of servant who could be politely ignored. Melanie's back almost arched. She said: 'No, I'm not modelling. I'm making tea.'

'How nice. Do you think I could have some, Ricky?'

Again it was perfectly calculated, implying that it was Ricky's tea, and that Melanie was merely there to pour it. Ricky looked embarrassed, then said: 'I'm sure Melanie won't mind getting you some.'

'I'll get it myself,' she said. 'We needn't trouble Melanie. You ought to get someone to repair your bell, dear. I've been trying to ring for half-an-hour. And someone bolted the door, so I couldn't reach through and open it. I shouted till I was quite hoarse, then had to go to the basement.'

She was pulling off her gloves, and staring at me curiously as she said this. Ricky introduced us.

'Celia — this is Harry, a new tenant.'

I had a feeling that Celia couldn't care less who I was. But to my surprise she shook my hand cordially, and said: 'Which room are you in?'

'The one to the right of the front door.'

'That's useful. If I find the door locked again, I can always knock on your window, can't I?'

'With pleasure,' I said, flattered by her friendliness.

Melanie could contain herself no longer, and said: 'If you want to know, *I* locked the door. Ricky is trying to work. He said he was sick of being interrupted.'

'Poor boy,' Celia said. 'It must be rather difficult to be a landlord and a painter at the same time. You ought to come and live at our place. We've got that beautiful attic with the great skylight windows. You wouldn't get any interruptions there.'

'Only one,' Melanie said cattily.

'Oh no. I'd be a very efficient protector. Why don't you, Ricky?'

I went out to find Celia a cup; the spectacle of Melanie's fury was beginning to make me nervous. I had a feeling that Celia's mink fur was going to be spoiled at any minute by the violent impact of a wet palette. But as I left the kitchen Melanie came out of the room, looking like a thundercloud. I bumped into her, then drew her back into the kitchen before she could rush off downstairs. She was almost in tears. I said the first thing that came into my head: 'Don't be angry. I'll get rid of her.'

'How?' She looked hopeful.

'I'll just sit around and refuse to go.'

'That's no good. Ricky says he wants to be left alone, but he lets his woman friends come in. I'm sick of trying to help him. *He* doesn't want her to go.'

'I'm sure he doesn't want her to stay,' I said. 'He was just telling me how much he appreciates your efforts to keep people away.'

'He was?' She looked more cheerful.

'Who is Celia anyway?' I asked.

She shrugged. 'She was Ricky's model and his mistress. Then she married a millionaire. Now she pretends she wants to help Ricky sell his paintings. But *I* know what she wants.' Her sense of grievance returned in full. 'Now she tries to make him go and live with her!'

'He won't,' I said. 'He was telling me that he'd hate to leave this place... and you.'

'He said he didn't want to leave me?'

I nodded. Then, to my delight, she put her arms round my neck and kissed me. She said: 'You are good.' I am sure she didn't believe me. But she realised I was sympathetic. I said: 'I'd better get back in there.'

'Make her go,' she said.

Celia was sitting on the table, swinging her legs, when I came in. It was hard to feel hostility towards her. In spite of her clothes, and a certain air of knowing how to get what she wanted, she had a delightful, impudent manner. She said: 'Ah, our chaperon's back. Close the door properly. Did she tell you to throw me out?'

181

I laughed, and busied myself with pouring her tea. Ricky said anxiously: 'Where's Melanie?'

'Listening outside the door,' Celia said.

'She's in the kitchen,' I said. I was about to sugar the tea, when the fine grain of the sugar halted me; I tasted it, and discovered that it was salt. In the few moments before she went out, Melanie had succeeded in switching the sugar. I soon located it among the still-life objects on the table.

Celia was saying: 'I don't know why you pay so much attention to that child. How old is she, fourteen?'

'Sixteen.'

'Mmm. So they can't accuse you of technical rape.'

'You know damn well she's still a virgin.'

'Really? Then she's obviously hating every minute of it. Can't you oblige her?'

Ricky said patiently: 'You didn't come her to talk about Melanie.'

'No, dear. I came to seduce you.' I couldn't decide whether this was frankness or Celia's idea of repartee. Ricky said: 'You can't. I'm being virtuous. I'm going in for Beethoven and chastity.'

'It won't last long,' Celia said. She had been showing a disquieting expanse of leg; now she went over to Ricky, wound herself round him like a creeper, and pressed her mouth to his. I quickly slipped the catch on the door and locked it; I knew that if Melanie walked in Ricky's popularity would slump to zero. Ricky gave the impression of merely standing there and allowing himself to be kissed, but from the way Celia's thighs pressed against him I could see she was enjoying it. Then she released him, sat down again on the table, and said with serene conviction: 'You're sex-starved.'

'My reactions are normal,' Ricky said, taking up a paintbrush. But I thought his voice sounded breathless. I had a feeling that, if I left the room, Melanie's worst apprehensions would be justified. Celia looked at me and grinned.

'Are we embarrassing Harry?'

'Not at all. I was just hoping you'd give me your opinion on whether I'm sex-starved too.'

'Not now. I'll come and see you in your room.'

The doorknob was tried; then someone knocked. Ricky shouted: 'Who is it?'

'Me — Eric.'

I unlocked the door, and Eric Primrose came in. Celia didn't look particularly pleased to see him. He said: 'Hello, dear — slumming again?'

She said: 'Hello, pieface. Still wearing that gardenia perfume?'

Eric said: 'No, it's me Russian cigarettes.' He pulled several long black cigarettes out of the top pocket of his pearl-grey jacket. 'Present from King Farouk.'

'How did you get in?' Ricky asked him. 'Didn't you find the door locked?'

'No, I've been here for hours, in Vera's room. Melanie just came in and said you'd made some tea, so I thought I'd join you.'

I realised that, although Melanie had temporarily retreated, she had her own guerilla method of harassing Celia.

Eric placed one hand on Ricky's shoulder and said: 'Don't worry, dear, I shan't seduce him. My admiration's purely intellectual, isn't it, maestro?'

'I hope so,' Ricky said gravely. It was obvious to me that he was thinking of other things.

'You're looking harassed today,' Eric said seriously. 'Are you feeling all right?'

'I'm O.K.,' Ricky said abstractedly, staring at the canvas. Then he seemed to become aware of the rest of us, and said, 'I must work. I'm not working hard enough.' I was aware that this was his way of hinting that he wanted to be left alone. For my own part, I was willing enough to leave; I wanted to move into my new room. But I wanted to leave in such a way that the other two would take the hint and come with me.

Eric said: 'I expect you're getting tired of being chased by sex-starved females. It must be quite exhausting.'

'You ought to know,' Celia said.

'I'm not sex-starved, dear,' Eric said sweetly.

Ricky said: 'My children, can't I persuade you to go and quarrel in Vera's room? Much as I love you both, I *must* get down to work.'

'Sorry, maestro,' Eric said, moving towards the door. 'Come and have some tea downstairs, Celia.' This, of course, was what Melanie had sent him in for. I could see that Celia's temper was running short.

'I came to ask you something,' she said glaring at Eric.

'Go ahead and ask, my pet,' Ricky said. He had taken up his brush again. 'Or is it very private?'

'I don't suppose so,' she said, shrugging. 'I've got a model for you.'

'I don't need a model,' Ricky said. 'I've got Narendra. Besides, I've got no money.'

'You don't need money. This girl wants to do it for fun.'

'I don't want to paint girls any more.'

'You let Melanie pose for you.'

'I know. She'd play hell if I had another model.'

'That's an excellent reason for getting another model.'

Eric asked curiously: 'Why the philanthropy? Has she got buck teeth and bandy legs?'

'You shut up,' Celia snapped. 'She's an extremely attractive girl, if you want to know.'

'Curiouser and curiouser,' Eric said.

'Who is she anyway?' Ricky asked.

184

'She's my sister-in-law's secretary — a rather sweet girl called Barbara. You'd like her. She's the wide-eyed, innocent type. Pre-Raphaelite virgin.'

'I don't like virgins,' Ricky said. 'If they're over eighteen, they're emotionally frustrated.'

'Quite. And *if* she stays around our house, she *won't* be much longer.'

'Blimey,' Eric said. 'Your sister-in-law's like that, is she?'

'Not her, you fool.'

'Your husband?' Ricky said. 'I thought he was tame.'

'So did I. But he's a sucker for the innocent look. And this girl gets far too much free time. So I'm locking the stable door before the horse gets out.'

'Mmm. And what do you want me to do?'

'You can do what you like with her... the more the better.'

'I don't want to seduce *anybody*! Ricky said irritably. 'I'm too busy.'

'You don't *have* to, dear. Just let her make you tea and meet the crazy gang downstairs. Anything to keep her occupied. She's got romantic ideas about art and artists.'

'All right,' Ricky said. 'I'll try anything once.'

Celia kissed him, then patted him on the cheek.

'That's my sweet. I knew you wouldn't let me down.'

'I hope Melanie can be persuaded to let her in,' I said, beating a retreat towards the door.

'Whose side are you on?' Celia asked me.

'Everybody's,' I said, and went out. I began to understand why Ricky's life was so difficult. I decided that, if I ever became famous, I would go and live on a desert island.

During the next hour, I swept out my new room and swabbed the floor with a mop. I piled the odds and ends — presumably the Welshman's property — in the corner behind the lavatory, and then installed the camp bed and some blankets. There was a gas pipe in the corner, and I connected up a gas-ring. I discovered that this warmed the room effectively and quickly; the only difficulty was that it also made the air stifling.

When I finally went downstairs, I discovered that Doreen was home. When I broke the news that I had a room, she looked as if she didn't understand.

'Where?'

'Upstairs — opposite Ricky's room.'

'But what's wrong with this one?'

'There's nothing wrong with it. But it's your room. You might not want me around all the time.'

To my amazement, she sat down on the bed and began to cry. I put my arm round her and explained that I had no intention of deserting her. I gathered finally that it had been one of those days when everything goes wrong; she had been missing buses, losing handkerchiefs and forgetting her change, and had narrowly escaped being knocked down by a taxi. The news about the room was the last straw. It took me some time to convince her that I hadn't taken the room to try to escape from her. When I did, we had one of those reconciliations that taste somehow like the smell of clean air after a heavy shower. She became strangely affectionate and tender. She cooked me an enormous meal, then we switched off the light and lay down on the bed. Within five minutes, she was asleep. In the light of the fire, her face looked as serene as a baby's. I lay there watching her, my hand on her waist feeling the rise and fall of her breathing, and thought about Ricky and Melanie and Celia and the Welshman. It had been less than a fortnight since I left home to come to London, my head full of notions about learning the meaning of freedom. I wondered if the search for freedom inevitably finishes in a woman's bed.

Chapter Two

I WAS AWAKENED by the sound of tapping on the window. (Our window could be easily reached from the front doorstep.) I sat up dizzily, and listened. Then I peered at the clock. We had been asleep for three hours. Doreen said sleepily: 'What is it?' Someone knocked on the door. James's voice called: 'Anybody awake?' I ran my fingers through my hair, and opened the door. He said: 'Oh sorry. Did I wake you up?'

I saw he had a girl standing behind him. They were carrying several bottles. I said: 'Hold on a moment. Doreen's still asleep.'

'Who is it?' Doreen asked. She was sitting on the edge of the bed, zipping up her skirt. We both looked dopey with sleep. 'Don't let them in.'

I felt foolish and awkward, standing in stockinged feet. So I just stood back, and let James walk in. He said: 'Don't worry, dear. One of the disadvantages of being born with X-ray eyes is that you cease to notice when women are undressed. We bring you alcoholic offerings. Let me introduce you to Joan.'

The girl who had followed him in was by no means a beauty; but when she removed her coat I saw she had an overblown but very passable figure. We said hello. James explained: 'Joan is responsible for the wine.'

'I thought you were in Luton,' Doreen said.

'I'm playing truant from rehearsals. I've offered to introduce Joan to the splendours and miseries of our oversexed menagerie. I trust you hadn't retired for the night?'

I made an excuse to go upstairs. As I came out of the lavatory, I met James. He winked, and steered me into the bathroom.

'Sorry to burst in on you like this, old boy. First things first. Do you think Joan and I could have a corner of your floor to sleep on tonight?'

'I can do better than that. I've got a spare room upstairs. But there's only one bed in it.'

'Don't worry about that. I don't anticipate much sleep anyway. What do you think of Joan? Rather a monster, eh?'

'Quite attractive,' I said cautiously. 'But hardly your type.'

'Of course she's my type. Her father owns half Luton. He gives her an allowance of fifty quid a month. I can't quite make up my mind whether I ought to marry her and give her the privilege of supporting a great artist.'

'What does she do?'

'Part-time secretary. But she thinks she could be a painter. So I've offered to introduce her to Ricky. She's all anxious to live the Bohemian life.'

Vera looked round the bathroom door. She was carrying an armful of beer bottles.

'Hello, you two. Do you feel like contributing for some wine?'

'I can do better than that,' James said. 'I've brought a few bottles with me.'

'How many?'

'Four. I also have my source of supply with me, so we can get more. She wants to see the way artists live and love.'

'Good. Bring her up. I'll tell everybody to be specially dotty. Have you eaten?'

'I can always find room for a little caviare.'

When we got downstairs again, we found Doreen struggling to open a wine bottle with a broken corkscrew on a tin opener. James said: 'Never mind that, my dear. We'll attend to it upstairs.' He told the girl: 'We've been invited for supper.'

'Good. I'm ravenous.'

'Coming, Harry?'

'We'll join you in a moment,' I said.

When James and the girl had gone, we both climbed back into bed. Neither of us felt like precipitating ourselves into the middle of a party at short notice; sleep was too recently behind us. We heard more people arriving. Finally, I roused myself to comb my hair and brush the feathers off my trousers (the eiderdown leaked), and Doreen applied a little lipstick and changed her skirt for a pair of slacks. We dragged ourselves unwillingly upstairs.

Most of the usual crowd seemed to be present. Tilly and Robby were sitting on a bed, peeling potatoes on to a sheet of newspaper between their feet. There was an enormous cooking pot in the grate — the sort in which the witches are supposed to brew their poisons, but not so big. It was bubbling appetisingly over a roaring coal fire, filling the room with the smell of onions and gravy. Vera came out of the kitchen carrying a large tin, which she emptied into it. 'Pilchards,' she said. She peered into the depths of the cauldron, and then stirred it with a chunk of wood. At that moment Hoffmann came in the door; he was wearing a leather jacket with a sheepskin collar, and looked worn out. He was carrying a paper carrier bag.

'What have you brought?' Vera asked. He laid out his purchases one by one on the table, saying: 'Apples, stuffed olives, gruyère, lemon juice, garlic sausage.'

That'll improve it,' Vera said. She began opening parcels and pouring their contents into the cauldron. A great bag of apples made a splash that sent soup all over the room. When Hoffmann said: 'Don't put camembert in there — it's a waste,' she snapped: 'Shut up. I'm cook today.' She shook the camembert free of its clinging wrapping (its smell carried across the room)

189

and it plopped in. She gave the mixture a vigorous stir with the wood, then tasted it with a spoon. 'Not bad. Needs a bit more flavour.' She opened the bottle of lemon juice, and poured half into the soup. I was glad that I had not committed myself to joining the meal. I helped Doreen to wine; she leaned over and whispered that she intended to slip off as soon as she could. I felt the same. Three hours' sleep is the worst possible preparation for a party.

When the soup was bubbling like a swamp releasing its vapours, the middle-aged woman called Belladonna came in. She immediately became indignant on seeing the cooking pot.

'Where did you find that? It's mine.'

'We didn't know it was yours,' Vera said. 'I found it in the bathroom. Anyway, you're supposed to cook things in it.'

'That's not what I bought it for,' Belladonna said. It transpired that she had broken her chamberpot the day before, and had bought this replacement in the Portobello market. The explanation made everyone gloomy, and James's girl-friend Joan looked physically sick. The effect of her announcement soothed Belladonna's annoyance, so she admitted that she had only bought it that morning, and hadn't yet made use of it. Vera added that it had been full of dust, and that it had obviously been used last as a coal scuttle. Everybody was reassured; five minutes later, they were holding out their plates while Vera served the muddy-looking mixture, using a small saucepan as a ladle. James's girl-friend accepted some with cheerful politeness, but I watched her as she edged her way to the annexe and finally slipped it under a bed. (Appropriately enough, it was Belladonna's bed.)

Doreen went over to her and engaged her in conversation; within five minutes they were chattering like a sewing circle, while James cast occasional irritated glances towards them. His girlfriend may have wanted to see the 'arty set', but it was obvious that she was glad enough to find someone of her own sort. In fact, I think it was greatly to James's advantage that she went into a huddle with Doreen; otherwise I am certain she would have changed her mind about staying the night the moment she could think up a plausible excuse. I looked at her with a kind of pity. I knew her type: well-dressed, with a good figure, but no vitality, and the kind of face you would never look at twice. She could have been an infant-school teacher. I wondered if she realised what she was letting herself in for when she agreed to stay the night. (Apparently she did, for James told me later that she was not a virgin.) Whatever she wanted out of life, it had nothing in common with Vera and Belladonna and Hoffmann. (At this moment, Belladonna was telling everyone about her first abortion while they wolfed their soup; she was, I must admit, a funny raconteuse, and obviously a great favourite.)

As I sat there, with the murmur of Doreen and Joan in one ear and Belladonna's voice in the other, it came to me that I was completely out of it — out of both worlds. I felt much as James did about Joan and her bourgeois background. But I felt no kind of sympathy for the others in the room. They had a taste for the exotic, the unconventional; but apart from that they were bores and weaklings. But while I was thinking what a dreary lot they were I remembered Ricky upstairs, and felt more cheerful. Without people like Ricky, it would be easy to get nihilistic about the philosophy of Bohemia. But contempt is a form of moral suffocation; I try to run from the things that provoke it.

I whispered in Doreen's ear that I was going to our room, and then slipped out. (There was a door leading

191

out of the annexe on to the landing, but it was kept bolted on the inside — to avoid interruption when marijuana was being smoked, I presume.) When I got down to the hall, someone banged on the front door. I opened it; it was Oswald Blichstein, wearing the strange cross-eyed look that he acquires when drunk.

'Ah, my dear boy, how nice to see you.' He planted a wet kiss on my forehead, then turned and beckoned to someone in the street, shouting: 'C'mon in, children.'

'Who've you brought with you...' I started, when Eric's voice screamed: '*You* come and help us, you lazy pig.'

'I can't,' Oswald said. 'I don't belong to your union.'

I saw that a van had pulled up outside the gate, and two men seemed to be unloading something. Oswald put his arm round my shoulder, and patted me: 'You go and help them, dear boy. You have the muscles of a stevedore.' He pushed me gently down the steps. I went out to the van, and found that two men in shirt sleeves had already dragged a large box halfway out. On closer inspection I realised that the 'box' was a coffin. Eric was leaping from one foot to the other with agitation.

'Be careful. It's full of booze.' I lent a hand. It weighed several hundredweight. It was not too difficult to carry to the front door, but the stairs were a different matter. Eric and I got one on either side of it. The two men — hefty, red-faced Cockneys — only spoke to issue brief instructions (the only time I heard a complete sentence was when one muttered to the other: 'Roll on the revolution'). I suggested that we should dump it in my room for the time being, but Oswald shouted: 'Certainly not. It's to go up to Ricky's studio.' Hoffmann came out of the upstairs room to see what the noise was about, and summoned the other men. But the stairs were too narrow for any other helpers; we manhandled it up to the first landing. In the light it proved to be a polished redwood coffin with curves instead of angles. It had none of the usual bits of chrome and brass, and its handles were made of wood. It was the kind of coffin that Flaubert would have wanted to be buried in.

The flight of stairs up to Ricky's room was narrower than the one below, and it had more curves. I went up and knocked on the door. A girl's voice answered. I went in, and found Melanie sitting on the bed in her pants and bra, filing her toe-nails. Ricky was painting.

I said: 'You'd better get dressed — we're being invaded.'

Ricky said: "They're not coming up here, are they?'

Before he could answer, Oswald came in. He intercepted Melanie as she dashed for the screen and began to kiss her neck, lifting her clear of the floor, shouting: 'Delicious child. I've dreamed of this moment all my life!' When she pulled his hair, he let her go. She rushed behind the screen.

Ricky said sourly: 'What the hell do you want?'

'I have brought you a present, maestro.' He swept the still-life objects off the table as the men came in with the coffin. 'Put it here.'

Luckily, the table was capable of supporting a steam-roller; the men dumped the coffin on it, and then reeled back on to chairs, mopping off sweat with grubby hand-kerchiefs. Eric was saying to Ricky: 'I'm sorry about this, maestro, but I couldn't stop him. He saw the bloody thing in a shop in St. Pancras and just went in and bought it.'

Oswald said tipsily: 'Alexander had a slave who had to whisper, "Remember you are mortal," when he got too conceited. I have gone one better. I ordered a hearse, complete with coffin, to follow me around. However, the driver insisted on taking it home at seven o'clock, so I had to be content with a Bedford van. Allow me to make you a gift of it.'

'What the hell am I supposed to do with it?'

'Why not sleep in it like the phantom of the opera? It's plush lined.' He turned to one of the workmen: 'Gentlemen, you are not doing your duty.'

'Let me get me breff back,' one of the men said. He produced a screwdriver, and proceeded to take off the lid. Everybody in the room (that is, everybody in the house) crowded round. It was full of bottles, packed neatly in straw — champagne, whisky, gin, red wine — even some cider. A cheer went up. Oswald proceeded to open a bottle of champagne. The cork flew out with a loud explosion and shattered the window; a stream of champagne shot after it.

'Glasses!' Oswald shrieked, holding his hand over the bottle. 'In there.' I dug among the straw in the coffin and found rows of glasses, neatly wrapped in brown paper. I tore off the paper and started to hand them out. Another cork popped. Within five minutes everybody in the room was drinking, including the workman who had hoped for the imminent revolution.

I heard Ricky saying: 'Can't I persuade you to take everybody downstairs? I want to paint,' but no one heard him.

James said in my ear: 'Joan's eyes are so wide open that I think her eyelids have got jammed. She obviously thinks I've arranged all this for her benefit.' The girl was certainly looking much happier.

Music started up. Somebody had put one of Doreen's jazz records on Ricky's gramophone. Melanie came out from behind her screen, looking about ten years old in a black and white check dress. Oswald spotted her, and she hurriedly took shelter with me in a corner. She whispered: 'He is mad, no?'

Before I could answer, Oswald was with us, his arms round Melanie's waist. He said: 'Darling child, why did you get dressed? You look so much lovelier in your undies. It displays a bourgeois prudery that pains me.'

Melanie grabbed his arms and yanked them away, shouting: 'Will you please stop it!'

Oswald's eyes closed in ecstasy; 'Oh god, you look delicious — ravishing. Kiss me.'

Melanie said something indignant in French.

'I'll give you five pounds for a kiss,' Oswald said. He took out his wallet and held the note under her nose.

'You are serious?' Melanie said, her eyes wide. Oswald waved the note. She chuckled suddenly and snatched it, then kissed him; he clutched her to him and almost bent her over backwards. Melanie, the scrap of white paper clutched in her left hand, held on gamely.

Oswald let her go, shuddering. He said: 'Let's go to bed, my sweet. My soul is on fire.'

Melanie said something rude.

He pulled out his wallet and waved a bundle of notes. 'A hundred pounds. I'll give you a hundred pounds to come into the other room with me.'

She hit out furiously, and the notes went up in the air like confetti. Then she dashed under his arm and out of the room. (She was still clutching the five pounds, I noticed.)

Oswald said sadly: 'You wound my heart, *mignonne*, but I shall never cease to adore you.' I helped him gather up his money.

Ricky came over. He said: 'Look here, Oswald, it's kind of you to bring all this drink, but I don't want a party. Tell your workmen to take it all downstairs, there's a good bloke.'

Oswald looked at him uncomprehendingly, then grasped his arm, and said: 'Maestro, my heart is breaking, but I rejoice in your happiness. You have genius, maestro. I have too, but I'm too lazy to develop it.'

The door opened again, and one of the workmen

came in carrying a television set. He staggered over with it and asked, 'Where's this to go?'

'What in hell's this?' Ricky asked.

'Another present,' Oswald said. 'I think we'll have it in the same corner as the gramophone.' He led the man across the room, clearing a way through the crowd. Ricky said to me: 'I'm afraid he's gone off his rocker this time.' Eric came near us, and Ricky grabbed him.

'What's the matter with Oswald? Has he gone mad?'

'I just don't know. All I know is that he's been drunk since midday. He's being very mysterious. He keeps rambling on about that devil worshipper bloke... have you met him?'

'Roehmer? Yes. He came yesterday. I let him take a few paintings away with him.'

Oswald came back. He placed his hand on Ricky's shoulder, and said: 'Call me Judas, maestro. But don't forget that Christ owes his fame to Judas. If Judas hadn't betrayed his master, we shouldn't have had the crucifixion. No crucifixion, no resurrection. No resurrection, no Christianity. Judas was a mere cogwheel in the destiny of the god-man.'

'What are you babbling about?'

Vera came over with a tray of drinks. Oswald helped himself to one and said: 'Here's to betrayal. Your health, gentlemen.' He spotted Melanie in the doorway, and weaved his way towards her.

Ricky shrugged and drank his champagne. He said in my ear: 'Would you mind if I went down to your room? I can't stand all this racket.'

'Please do,' I said. 'But we're probably coming down in a few minutes.'

'That's O.K. I just want to escape this bear garden.'

The television came on, but without sound. It was a pop singer with a guitar; he was writhing his body and staring magnetically into the camera, but the silence gave his act an air of parody.

One of the workmen came over to me. 'Do you know where your mate's gone? We'd like to go if he's finished with us.'

I looked round for Oswald, then went out on the landing. The door of the next room was slightly ajar. I pushed it open, and saw Melanie being kissed by Oswald; she didn't seem to be protesting. I coughed and she broke away, her face pink.

'The workmen want to go,' I said.

Oswald groped in his pocket, pulled out two pound notes, and said: 'Oblige me, dear boy, by giving them that.'

I snatched the money and withdrew. The door closed again. I found the men and gave them the money. Then my eyes were drawn to the television screen. To my amazement, I saw the face of Sir Reginald Propter. I rushed to the table and tried to find the sound knob, but the first one I turned only made the picture fade. I went and banged on the door on the landing, shouting: 'Oswald, come and see to this TV set.' The door opened, and Melanie came flying out, her dress awry; she rushed into the lavatory without even looking at me. Oswald came behind her. I told him that Propter was on the television — a sort of foreboding told me that this was connected with the installation of the set.

He said: 'Really. Then my watch is slow.' He strode into the middle of the party, shouting: 'Quiet, everybody. Quiet, please. Where's Ricky? Go and get him, somebody.'

I flew down the stairs, taking four at a time, and found Ricky lying on my bed. 'Come on up, quick,' I said. He followed me without a word, sensing that something important was happening.

The room was in silence, except for the voice of the

197

television interviewer, who was saying: 'And now, Mr. Roehmer, would you mind telling us whether you agree with Sir Reginald about these remarkable paintings?'

A square, dead-white face flashed on the screen; Roehmer had a completely bald head (shaved, no doubt) and great black circles under his eyes. He reminded me of Boris Karloff playing Frankenstein's monster. He said in a clipped, German voice: 'No, I cannot agree entirely. I do not feel that Prelati's painting reveals a mystical approach. On the contrary, he seems to me to be preoccupied with formal organisation, like Ben Nicholson. This receding vista, for example...'

The camera switched to a painting; I recognised it immediately as the one that had stood on Ricky's mantelpiece. As the voice droned on, I looked at Ricky's face; he looked positively malevolent. He said: 'The bloody fool...' He looked round the room, but Oswald was nowhere in sight. For a moment, I suspected that he was embracing Melanie somewhere; then I saw Melanie standing near the door, looking as neat and pretty as ever, showing no signs of her recent wrestling match.

Ricky went over to Eric, who said hastily: 'Don't blame me. I don't know a thing about all this. Oswald says he'll be back later, when you've calmed down.'

The interviewer was summing up: 'Well, Sir Reginald, I think our viewers will agree that you've again shown your really astonishing power of spotting new and talented painters. I only regret that the painter himself couldn't be here with us in the studio tonight...'

Ricky strode to the set and pulled the plug out of the socket. Nobody in the room seemed to be aware of his irritation. Vera murmured: 'Congratulations, darling,' and Desmond said: 'That was a lovely piece of publicity.

Who fixed it?' Ricky made for the door, and Melanie flung her arms round his neck. 'Darrrleeng, you are famous now.'

'If that's what you call fame,' Ricky said quietly, freeing himself. He went out. Tilly said loudly (intending her voice to carry after him): 'Well, what's bitten him?' Everybody began talking. My own feeling was that Ricky was showing a streak of affectation. It was possible, of course, that he sincerely preferred to be without that kind of publicity. The discussion of his paintings had been stupid enough. But there was no need to behave like a Victorian matron who has been solicited by a drunk. This seemed to be the general feeling in the room.

Desmond said loudly: 'Well if you ask me, he's bloody lucky. Whoever arranged it did him a good turn.'

Only Eric showed a genuine disposition to defend Ricky. 'But they ought to have *told* him if they wanted to show his pictures on TV. He's got a perfect right to object.'

'Wish I could get a piece of publicity like that,' James said wistfully.

Somebody opened another champagne bottle. Eric suggested that we should all go downstairs in case Ricky wanted to return and paint. The coffin was now considerably lighter, so we got it into the room below without much effort. The phone in the hall began to ring; I went and answered it. A woman's voice asked for Ricky. I said he was out and asked if I could take a message. 'No, I'll ring back tomorrow. But if you happen to see him, would you say Molly rang, and congratulations on the programme?' As soon as I hung up, it rang again. This time is was a journalist.

'I hear you've got a coffin full of champagne there and you're having a celebration?'

I said this was true.

'Do you think Mr. Prelati would mind if we brought a cameraman over to get a picture?'

I explained that Ricky had gone out, but it was obvious that he didn't believe me.

'We'll come anyway, if you don't mind.'

I hung up. Before I could reach the door of my room it rang again. I recognised Sir Reginald Propter's voice. 'Did Ricky see the programme?'

'He did.'

'Is he annoyed?'

'I think so. He's gone out.'

'Oh dear... Do you think it's a bad thing?'.

'No. I suppose it's excellent publicity.'

'Of course it is. And what's more, I've already been approached by a rich American who wants to give Ricky an exhibition in New York. If he plays his cards properly, he can be a wealthy man.'

'I'll tell him when he comes back,' I said. I made a bolt for my door as soon as I replaced the receiver; even so, it began to ring before I could get into the room. I ignored it, and closed the door behind me. I had half-expected to find Ricky or Oswald there, but the room was empty. Someone came downstairs and took the call. A moment later, I heard Tilly's voice shout: 'It's the *Daily Worker*. Is it true that Ricky won't exhibit because he disapproves of capitalist society?'

Hoffmann's voice called: 'I'll come and talk to them.' Since the phone was outside my door, I had no way of escaping the noise. I considered retreating to my top-floor lavatory, then remembered that James might already be there. I had to resign myself to the racket. I heard Hoffmann explaining that Ricky had gone out, and that he wasn't expected back until tomorrow. This struck me as rather decent of Hoffmann; he obviously wanted to save Ricky from being badgered. A moment later there was a knock on my door and Hoffmann came in.

'Who were the other calls from?'

I told him briefly. His eyes glittered with excitement.

'Did Propter tell you the name of this millionaire who wants to take Ricky to New York?'

I explained that Propter had not said the man was a millionaire, only a 'rich American', and that he hadn't offered to take Ricky to New York, only to exhibit his paintings there. He brushed these corrections aside impatiently.

'That's all right. You didn't tell this to the journalist bloke?'

'No. Propter rang afterwards.'

'Good. Well, keep it quiet. Don't tell anybody. Do you happen to know where I can find Propter?'

I said I didn't. Hoffmann was already dropping pennies into the coin box. I heard him say: 'Hello, give me the news desk... Hello, Jack, this is Ted Hoffmann. I've got a story. Right? Get this down. Following a television programme in which some of his paintings were shown, artist Ricky Prelati finds himself suddenly famous tonight... Got that? Prelati is sometimes known among his friends as the Greta Garbo of the art-world, because of his unwillingness to exhibit his work...'

James came in and asked if he could borrow a couple of cushions to use as pillows.

'How's Joan feeling?' I asked.

'Nearly gibbering with excitement. She's really had her money's worth tonight. She's drunk about a gallon of champagne. I think it's time we went to bed...'

As he opened the door, we heard Hoffmann saying: 'Send a photographer round if there's one to spare. We might as well get a picture. The *Daily Echo's* already sending a cameraman round...'

James returned the cushions to the armchair.

'On second thoughts, I think I'll stay up for a while. It looks like being fun.'

'It looks as if I shan't get any sleep,' I said gloomily.

'Don't be selfish, my dear Harry. Think of Ricky's luck.'

'He doesn't seem to think he's lucky.'

'He will. There's no such thing as a man who doesn't want to be famous.'

The doorbell rang, and James went. It was a reporter from the *Daily Echo* with a photographer. They all went upstairs, and the place was blessedly quiet for a few minutes. I decided to switch out the light to discourage further visitors; then I lay down on the bed. Someone tapped on the window and made me jump. I pushed aside the curtain and looked out on the front steps. There was no one there. So I opened the other window. Ricky's voice came from below: 'Is anybody about?'

'Not in here.'

'Good. Do you mind if I come in?'

'All right. But some reporters have just arrived.' He groaned: 'Oh Christ. That's fixed it.' I made sure there was no one in the hall or on the stairs, and let him in. He bolted into my room, and I locked the door behind us.

'Where's Melanie?' he asked.

'Still upstairs.'

'I think I'll have to stay the night at her place. I don't want to face that crowd tonight.'

'You'll have to face them some time, though, won't you?' We were sitting in the dark, only the fire lighting the room, and talking in whispers. Then we heard someone coming downstairs. Our door was rattled. 'Who is it?' I called. Doreen's voice answered, so I let her in. 'What are you doing here?' she asked Ricky. 'They're waiting to take pictures of you upstairs.'

'I know. Do you two want to get to bed? I can go.' We assured him that he was welcome to stay all night if he wanted to. Doreen asked: 'But why don't you see them and get it over with?'

'Because I'd be bloody rude. I could murder that fucking Oswald and his treacherous friends. What a filthy trick. This man Roehmer said he'd like to borrow some of my paintings to decorate the walls of his flat — just until I can paint some murals. Then look what the swine does...'

'But they only wanted to help you,' Doreen said.

'Help themselves to the credit of saying they discovered me,' Ricky said with disgust.

'But if your work's good, you'll be discovered sooner or later. Why try to put it off?'

'Because I'm not ready yet.'

'But what difference will it make?' Doreen persisted. 'It will only mean that people take an interest in your work. That won't prevent you from developing.'

'I know it won't,' Ricky said. 'Because I shan't let it. But it'll double my work.'

'Why?'

'Why? Don't you know anything about the art world? Do you think they simply want to encourage me? You're wrong. They only want to involve me in the game. I've seen it happen. You ought to meet Davis and Jones — the two Welsh painters who used to be in this room. Or Darrell Saunders. Did you ever come across Darrell? He had his first exhibition five years ago, and *The Times* said he was the best English landscape painter since Paul Nash. He made three thousand pounds from that exhibition. For six months he got nothing but praise. Then a few critics started to say he was over-rated, and an American art magazine published a long article attacking him. He tried to sue them for libel. His second exhibition got bad notices, and he started to drink. He hasn't painted anything worth looking at for three years, but he has a press cutting agency which sends him every single comment that's made about him in the newspapers.'

Someone came downstairs, and we realised that Ricky had been raising his voice. We all sat there in the dark. Someone knocked on the door, and James's voice called: 'Harry.'

'I'm in bed,' I shouted.

'Sorry, old boy. Can I have my cushions?'

I opened the door a fraction and thrust them round. I said: 'Leave the front door open for this other lot of reporters. I don't want to get out of bed.'

'I understand perfectly, Harry. Hope I didn't — ahem — interrupt you. Goodnight, old boy.'

I sat down again, and we resumed the discussion in whispers. Doreen said: 'I still don't see that you can judge yourself by other people. Your friend Darrell sounds rather weak.'

'I'm not judging myself,' Ricky said, 'I'm judging the bloody art world and the critics. If I'd learned how to say what I've got to say, it wouldn't worry me. I'd go ahead and say it, and the critics could go and shoot themselves if they didn't like it. But I'm still learning to say it. And I don't want a lot of people looking over my shoulder and offering impertinent opinions on how I ought to paint.'

'You're not interested in money and fame, then,' I asked.

'Of course I am — to some extent. But I don't need money at the moment. I've got enough to live. All I want is a studio and some canvases, and plenty of free time.'

Although I knew it was pouring oil on the flames, I couldn't resist telling him that Hoffmann had described him as 'the Greta Garbo of the art-world'. He swore so loudly that we both had to quieten him.

'You see what I mean!' he said. 'If I try to avoid publicity, I'm playing at being Greta Garbo. In other words, it's just another publicity gimmick. Can you see why I feel like vomiting?'

'All the same,' Doreen said stubbornly, 'it can't be as unpleasant as all that. It must be rather nice to know that you're a successful painter.'

Ricky stood up and placed his hand on Doreen's shoulder.

'My dear girl, I've never had the faintest doubt that I'd be successful. When I was sixteen, I met a weird Irish painter who was supposed to have second sight. He took one look at me, and said: "You're going to be very successful one of these days." And I replied: "Yes, I know." Because quite suddenly I realised I *did* know. I've always known it. It was only later that I began to realise what success can do to a man who's not prepared for it. So I determined I'd hold it off until I *was* prepared for it. I haven't succeeded.'

Neither of us could think of any comment. He loosened the catch and opened the door.

'I'm going over to Melanie's for the night. Don't tell anybody where I've gone. See you tomorrow.'

As he went out of the front door, I remembered Propter's phone call. I opened the window, and gave him the message about the rich American. All he said was: 'Oh god, that'd be the last straw.' A car pulled up outside. He dodged across the garden, and made for the side gate. I closed the window and started to undress, feeling strangely disheartened.

Doreen was peering out of the window. 'More photographers,' she said. 'Don't you think it's exciting?'

'I suppose so.'

'It makes you feel rather envious, in a way, doesn't it?' But it was not envy that kept me silent. I was trying to look into myself, and see if I could discover there the same absolute certainty of future success. What I discovered worried me. It was the realisation that there is no such thing as future success. It is either there all the time, or it is non-existent. But I had no criterion for recognising it.

Chapter Three

I FOUND IT so difficult to sleep that I finally agreed to take one of Doreen's sleeping tablets; this laid me out like a blow on the head, and I slept dreamlessly until morning. The noise of the phone woke me, but I was still half-drugged, and drifted for another hour in a light sleep that seemed to be punctuated with the sound of bells. It was about ten o'clock when I finally struggled unwillingly back to consciousness, and found Doreen making tea.

'Ricky's back. He wants you to help him with something. And Sir Reginald Propter's coming over, and Ricky says he won't see him.'

The morning sunlight made our room a totally different place. It was admittedly dusty, and the walls needed redecorating. Yet there was something very cheerful about the sounds that came from outside. It was ten paces to the pub, ten paces to the grocer across the road, and only fifteen minutes from Portobello Market. On a dreary day you might feel trapped in bricks and mortar. But on a sunny morning you felt close to the centre of life in a way that peaceful suburb-dwellers never know. Grimy children played outside (and often climbed the tree in front of our window); navvies in shirtsleeves ate their meals at the workmen's café two doors away. It was true that the place had no air of innocence. The back garden received its share of used contraceptives every night. By walking a quarter of a mile in almost any direction, you could pass gangs of young toughs — either local lads or coloured immigrants — who carried razors and coshes. The square mile round our house had had a high percentage of murders, solved and unsolved, and in the winter of 1955 the names of Heath and Christie were still recent memories in Notting Hill. Altogether, it is the kind of area to whose description certain modern novelists would enjoy bringing an air of brooding evil, of irredeemable sin and misery. This would be possible if you ignored the curious and vital pulse of the place, which is immoral and almost inhuman, but certainly not evil.

I drank my tea, my back propped against the wall, and watched the dust floating through the sunlight.

'Have you seen James yet?'

'Yes, they're awake. More tea?'

She had strung a line over the fireplace; I watched her draping handkerchiefs on it. She was wearing an apron, and rubber gloves to keep her hands dry. The housewife appearance amused me. I said: 'Do you think Joan makes a habit of sleeping with strange men?'

'I'm sure she doesn't.'

'And do you approve of all this promiscuity?'

'No. I think they're a stupid lot. They quite amuse me, but I couldn't bear to live like that.'

'Then why are you sharing a room with me?'

'Because you're not one of them.'

The phone rang. She said: 'Damn. That phone's been ringing all morning.' She went to answer it, and I stared out of the window. I could see what she meant. A great many things had happened to me in the past fortnight. But I was certain of one thing: I could never live according to James's 'philosophy of freedom'. For better or worse, I am a bourgeois.

She came back in. 'Somebody else wanting to speak to Ricky. He says he won't speak to anybody.' The front door bell rang. I peered out past the curtain. It was Propter. Doreen let him in. I hastily pulled on some trousers while he was still outside.

'Morning, Harry. Is Ricky back?'

'He is. But Doreen tells me he's in a bloody mood.'

Doreen handed him a cup of tea. He said, sighing: 'I wish he wouldn't make it so difficult to help him.'

'I'm afraid he doesn't think you have helped him.' I paraphrased, as best I could, the comments Ricky had made on the subject. To do Propter justice, I think he saw Ricky's point of view.

'I can see that he might get annoyed about the kind of thing the critics say... but it doesn't have to be all attacks. Anyway, I think Ricky's painting is far more developed than he realises. If he died tomorrow, he'd still be regarded as an important talent, on the strength of his work up to date. Perhaps I'd better go and talk to him.'

Doreen said: 'I'm afraid he's... he says he doesn't want to see anybody.'

'Couldn't you talk to him, Harry?'

'I could. But I'm not sure that he's not right.'

'He may be indeed,' Propter said good humouredly. 'Unfortunately, it's done now. The problem is simply to get him to co-operate.'

I said nothing, but started in on a boiled egg. Propter shrugged and said: 'Ah well, we can leave that problem until later. What about the work you wanted?'

'Work?' I said. In this house, the word seemed foreign. 'Oh, you mean the advance you paid me?'

'I've just bought a small publishing firm. How would you like to work for me?'

'I don't know. What would it involve?'

'Not very much to begin with. I plan to publish worthwhile religious and philosophical works. And, of course, any talented young writers I discover... It wouldn't be a full time job. You'd have to read manuscripts that came in, read proofs and so on. For, say, three days a week.'

I could hardly believe my luck. I tried not to look too eager.

'It sounds splendid,' I said cautiously. 'When do I start?'

'You'd better come tomorrow. I'm using a room in my house as an office at present.'

I caught Doreen's eye as she removed the cups, and saw that she was as delighted as I was. As she went out, she said: 'Harry, why don't you go and talk to Ricky?'

'I suppose I could.'

'See what you can do,' Propter said.

Under the circumstances, I could hardly refuse. So I made my way up to Ricky's room. His door was locked: when I rattled the handle he shouted: 'Who is it? I'm working.'

'Harry.'

He opened the door.

'Ah, good. Come on in.' He locked it again. 'What's happening down there?'

'People keep ringing up to speak to you.'

'I know. I got some of the messages. People I haven't seen or spoken to for years have been ringing me up. And three art galleries have offered me exhibitions.'

He sat down on the bed, and sipped something from an enormous mug. (It was a glucose drink that he drank in huge quantities when painting.) I could see, from the state of his palette, that it was not true that he was working.

'Propter's downstairs,' I said.

'I hope you told him I want to tear out his entrails?'

'I think he gathered that. He still wants to see you.'

'It's no good. I just don't want to see him. I can't face anybody this morning.'

'What did you want to see me about?'

'Ah yes. I've got an idea to put to you. I told Melanie's mama that I'd probably have to leave this place. She got quite worried, because she likes to have somebody reliable around to stop the tenants from burning the banisters or tearing up the floorboards. So I suggested you might keep an eye on the place.'

'I wouldn't mind. But where do you want to go to?' He shrugged. 'Anywhere where I can paint in peace.' 'Couldn't you barricade yourself in this place?' He looked up and stared at me. 'You've got an idea there.' He unlocked the door and went out on to the landing. 'If I could make a door on the stairs, and cover in this part with a sheet of hardboard...' He stuck his hands in his pockets. 'The trouble is, it would cost twenty quid to do it properly, and I haven't got twenty quid.'

'Get it off Propter,' I said. 'After all, it's his fault.'

'That's an idea. Why shouldn't he? Where is he now?'

'Down in my room. Shall I go and ask him?'

'Bring him up. Find out first if he's got any money on him.'

I hurried downstairs, delighted with the solution. Propter was staring moodily out of the window while Doreen made the bed. 'Any luck?' he asked.

'I think so.' I outlined Ricky's idea to him. 'Good. That's easy enough. Are you sure he wants to see me, though?'

'He said so.'

I could feel Propter's apprehension as he followed me upstairs. (Anybody would think twice before annoying a man of Ricky's size.) But Ricky was actually grinning when we found him. He was measuring the stairs with a folding rule. All he said to Propter was: 'You're a nice kind of pest, aren't you?'

'I'm sorry. But you know the reason I did it without consulting you.'

'All right. Forget it. It's done now. Do you still want to buy one of my paintings?'

'Of course.'

'Good. I'm going to turn this place into a fortress. I'm going to build a door across the stairs. If that doesn't work, I'll set mantraps on the stairs and keep two hungry Alsatians chained to the banisters. Have you got any money on you?'

Propter produced his wallet, and extracted a wad of notes. 'How much do you need?'

'About twenty-five quid, for the moment.'

The money was handed over, Ricky said: 'Look at my paintings in here and see if there's anything you want. Come on, Harry.'

This was typical Ricky. As soon as he conceived an idea, he had to put it into operation. We visited a wood merchant in the next street, and Ricky ordered great chunks of timber and huge areas of hardboard. I went and borrowed the handcart from my friend the junk merchant, and we finally transported the stuff back to the house. It took us most of the morning to get it all up to Ricky's studio. We cleared the centre of the room, then began sawing and hammering. Even Propter did something to help, holding the beams in place while Ricky and I drove in nails. We constructed a solid timber frame across the stairs, then attached the door (bought complete from the hardware shop). I left Ricky to screw on the lock while I went for a meal. When I went back after lunch he had completed the job, and it would have been impossible to get on to the upper landing without either breaking the door or risking breaking your neck by clambering up the outside of the banisters. He handed me the spare key. 'You'll need this to get to your room.' (He meant my lavatory.)

'Has Propter gone?'

'I sold him my "Downfall of Civilisation" for seventy-five quid. He's given me a cheque for the rest. Call Doreen up, and come and have a drink.'

The three of us retreated ceremoniously behind the new door, and Ricky pushed home two bolts. Once behind it, it was impossible to see down the stairs, for Ricky had constructed great screens around the landing. We went into Ricky's room, and he opened a bottle of Beaune. 'Here's to privacy,' he said. We all drank.

'That reminds me,' Doreen said. 'About ten people called this morning. I told them you were out.'

'Good girl. From now on, I'm always out. In fact, I no longer live here.'

I refilled my glass, and felt a warm glow spreading in my veins. It was one of those complex things that spring out of satisfied vanity, the glow of achievement, and a feeling of having discovered something real and permanent. It was flattering that Ricky should want to escape from everybody else, and yet had accepted Doreen and myself as allies. It pleased my vanity to feel that Doreen was in this position because she had met me. But, sitting there, I had an intuition that I had met two people who would occupy a permanent place in my life. It was not merely a warm glow of fellowship, accompanied by a premonition. It was like discovering something that was already present inside me. There was a strange familiarity about the situation, as if I had already looked back on it a hundred times from the future.

As we refilled the glasses, the doorbell rang twice. Two rings was Ricky's signal. We ignored it. It rang again: — an uncertain ring, timid yet persistent. I went to the window and looked down.

'Girl in a green beret,' I said. 'Fawn raincoat.'

Doreen said: 'Oh damn, I forgot to tell you. A girl named Barbara rang to say she's coming this afternoon. I expect that's her.'

'Barbara? I don't know any Barbara. Tell her I'm not at home.'

'She mentioned someone called Celia and said she'd promised to model for you.'

Ricky clutched his forehead.

'Oh god, I remember. Celia's little secretary girl. We'd better let her in.' Doreen went out. Ricky looked at me with an expression of agony and resignation.

'Here we go again,' he said.

Available from New London Editions

Available

Baron's Court, All Change by Terry Taylor
(introduction by Stewart Home)

King Dido by Alexander Baron
(introduction by Ken Worpole)

October Day by Frank Griffin
(introduction by Andy Croft)

Rain on the Pavements by Roland Camberton

Rosie Hogarth by Alexander Baron
(introduction by Andrew Whitehead)

Scamp by Roland Camberton
(introduced by Iain Sinclair)

The Furnished Room by Laura Del-Rivo

Forthcoming

This Bed My Centre by Pamela Hansford Johnson
(introduction by Zoë Fairbairns)

Available from bookshops or www.fiveleaves.co.uk